PEDRATERRA
&
ANGLETERRE

.

Two Fables

PEDRATERRA
&
ANGLETERRE

·

Two Fables

BY

ANTHONY RUDOLF

Odd Volumes

of the
Fortnightly Review

LES BROUZILS
2021

Odd Volumes of

The Fortnightly Review

www.fortnightlyreview.co.uk

Editorial office:
Château Ligny
2 rue Georges Clemenceau
85260 Les Brouzils
France

ODD VOLUMES 2021

ISBN 978-0-9991365-8-4

For Paula and to the memory of Kitaj

Thanks to several friends who read drafts of the story, especially Karl Stead
Thanks to Chip Martin for discussions about Los Angeles etc
Thanks to Cathie Pilkington and Robin Smart for technical advice

Cathie Pilkington's print which accompanies 'Pedraterra' is
available from Red Breast Editions www.redbreasteditions.com

Acknowledgements to Faber and Faber, who published Clarence
Ellis, *The Pebbles on the Beach, in 1954.*

CONTENTS

PEDRATERRA

PART ONE:
LOS ANGELES

1.

Peter and Gemma, my daughter's son and my son's daughter, are my grandchildren. She lives in London, he lives in Dunedin. I live half-way between the two, in Westwood, Los Angeles.

I send them emails and funny postcards. Together, they bring out the child in me, which is not difficult.

They send each other Skypes at opposite ends of the day. They play chess:

"Peter, pay attention. Forget about the Rubik Cube. It's your move".

Peter tests out his new conjuring tricks. Gemma displays her pastels and digital drawings.

2.

In Westwood, I walk to the Coffee Bean where I do my writing. Away from the computer, I am less tempted to side-track. My toys stay in the pram.

Arriving at 8 in the morning, I greet my painter friend Craig, He's here every day from 6 before going to his studios to work.

— Good morning, Dunstan, late bird.

— Good morning, Craig. My grandchildren arrive today.

— Maybe I'll put them in a picture.

— Lovely thought. A final *latte*?

He leaves for his studio. I start work, on my lined, yellow legal pads.

3.

L/A Airport: Peter arrives at 1045, Gemma is due at 1445. Here he is, taller and thinner than before, curly hair longer, wearing a tee-shirt with a pebble on it.

Peter is still shy. He seems to wear masks. Gemma is more assertive. We hug.

— We have time on our hands till Gemma arrives. Let's drive to Venice beach and swim. That way you'll keep awake.

— Good id*eee*a, Grandpa. In New Zealand, we drive on the other side of the road.

4.

— Look at the surfers, grandpa.

— Race you to the sea.

— I won.

— Only just. What's not here, Peter?

— What do you mean, what's not here?

— Pebbles, there are no pebbles on this beach.

— Oh yes, not like Aramoana.

Cool sea water sweeps away his jetlag for the time being. Dried off, we eat ice-cream and return to the airport.

5.

The cousins hug. Gemma too has grown, filled out a little. Her tee shirt sports a dinosaur. Gemma is speeding, about to take off. In the car they announce they have presents for me, pebbles of course, Gemma's from Brighton, Peter's from Aramoana, where once he saw a seal. Peter tells Gemma there were no pebbles on the beach.

We arrive in Westwood. Passing the Coffee Bean, I'm reminded of Craig, the painter they're going to meet. I'll phone him.

6.

The mess in my flat amazes the children. I tell them that when I lived in London my mother said half my stuff was rubbish. Yes mother, but which half? Sort out my life! Sort out my flat!

I show them their beds and then it is time to give them a meal and tell them about the special room, whose secret will be revealed tomorrow.

7.

Before dinner, they look at three pictures in my sitting-room, all black and white. I explain that Craig's work includes lithographs, images printed from drawings. They can be coloured or black and white. Craig makes five or ten copies. We'll visit the studio and learn how it's done. There are more prints in my bedroom, Bible characters.

8.

I'm sure you know
some of these stories:
Jacob and the pillow

of stone, Moses
striking the rock,
David killing Goliath,

Ruth the gleaner
whom we find in
one of the greatest

poems in the language:
'Ode to a Nightingale'
by John Keats.

I know it by heart
and will recite it to you
next time we're driving.

9.

I take them to
the room with a secret,
I unlock the door.

The children gasp,
order – so unlike
the chaos in other rooms:

shelves filled with pebbles
each one perching
on a numbered label.

The children notice
two texts on the wall:
a found poem

in prose from
The Pebbles on the Beach
by Clarence Ellis.

The cycle goes endlessly and steadily on. The finest grains become compacted into solid rock. Millions of years later the encroaching sea, aided by sun, wind and rain, breaks up the rock. A pebble is born. The waves roll it along the beaches from Cornwall to Sussex. It is resolved into sand grains and then the whole process starts again and another cycle of millions of years begins once more.

10.

Underneath Ellis,
another poem,
my own: I speak:

>*The Waves*
>They sweep away pebbles,
> seaweed, sand.

>The tide recedes. Movement
>of pebble is nothing.

>There are limits, after all
>the beaches.

Then I recite
two lines from another
poem of mine:

>I live on the edge, on edge.
>I balance on a pebble.

Life is a balancing
act I explain,
you weigh choices

and balance on a pebble
before deciding,
let's see:

shall I become a vegan?
Or what shall we have for dinner?
They hop round the room.

11.

They want me to tell them about my collection. I explain I used to be a travel agent and hotel inspector. I travelled the world and every day, before or after work, went to beaches where I found pebbles.

Later I had other jobs: security guard, swimming teacher, freelance translator, painter's model. Finally: writer.

12.

I invite them to tell me
what they notice
about the pebbles

— Some are perfectly round.
— Some are coloured.
— Like lithographs.

— They come in different sizes
I quote from *The Pebbles*
on the Beach,

> If pebbles happened to be identical in shape,
> they would almost certainly differ in texture,
> colour, surface pattern, degree of hardness
> or the nature of the rocks from which they
> originated.

If pebbles could talk
would we understand
their language?

— "Texture, colour, surface, hardness", says Peter,
in a pebble voice, quoting the author.

— You sound like a duck.

— Of course, how else would pebbles speak?

Before I can think of a reply, Peter says, "Look". He has spotted a door in the wall of the room, facing the one we came through. It is next to the window. He asks me to open the window; he looks out: nothing but the outside wall. He tells Gemma to look and holds on to her while she leans out of the window.

— A blank wall. What is the door for?

— Yes, what is it for? Is it a kind of painting or sculpture?

— You mean, is it what people call conceptual art?

— What's conceptual art?

— It's art where idea matters more than image.

— But this isn't an idea.

— It's a door.

— Which leads nowhere.

13.

I tell them
I'm going to prepare
fresh spaghetti

for lunch
and they will find
plenty to do in the garden.

After lunch
we'll talk about pebbles
and go to a museum.

Then we'll visit
Craig's studio
and after dinner....

— the door.

— the door.

— Yes, the door.

14.

Thanks to the camera
and microphone on the roof
I see and hear

the children on my smart phone.
They play table tennis,
jump on the trampoline,

take turns on the swing.
They play chess
on the limestone board

Carved by a friend.
— You're in check.
— I'm hungry.

I join them in the garden,
Gemma is winning.
— Grub's up.

15.

After leaving a message
on Craig's answerphone
I serve up spaghetti

Then back in the pebble room,
more Clarence Ellis,
some words can be rolled

round our mouths
like pebbles.
Repeat after me:

— Igneous, limestone, flint, marble, metamorphic,
rock, sandstone, pebble. Pebble.

Do you know the nonsense
verse of Edward Lear
and his limericks?

> The pobble who has no toes
> Had once as many as we.

— I like the limericks, which he illustrated himself. Lear made wonderful colour lithographs of birds. He was a rare example of a person who doubled as a writer and visual artist, like William Blake or Victor Hugo, who wrote *Les Misérables*.

— A limerick is a funny poem with five lines, says Peter.

— That's right, but Lear's rhymes are different from most people's. The rhyme in line one or line two is repeated in line five. Most people make a new rhyming word. Here's one of Lear's limericks.

> There was an Old Man who said "Hush!
> I perceive a young bird in this bush!"
> When they said, "Is it small?"
> he replied, "Not at all!
> It is four times as big as the bush!"

— Bush and hush don't rhyme properly, says Gemma.

— Quite right, unless "hush" is pronounced as in the north of England. But it looks like a rhyme when you write it down. I'll recite two limericks I wrote the other day.

There was an old poet called Lear
whose life was afflicted with fear.
He thought he'd gone mad
or perhaps he was bad,
so he lay down and shed a big tear.

I went on a tube train with Auden
from Totteridge/Whetstone to Morden.
He told me the tale
(called "Hammer and Nail")
of a captive and old jail warden.

— Those are better than Lear's, grandpa.

— Thank you, Peter. His best poem is 'The Owl and the Pussy-Cat'. Let's listen to two versions on YouTube: first, Igor Stravinsky's, followed by Burl Ives.

The Owl and the Pussy-cat went to sea
In a beautiful pea-green boat,
They took some honey, and plenty of
   money,
Wrapped up in a five-pound note.

They dined on mince, and slices of quince,
Which they ate with a runcible spoon;
And hand in hand, on the edge of the sand,
They danced by the light of the moon.

— What's a runcible spoon? asks Peter.

— I think Lear invented it. Come to my office, check it out in Google.

— Yes, Edward Lear did invent it, says Gemma.

— One of its meanings is "a fork which is also a spoon". Run-ci-ble: half-rhyme with pebble, and now, back to the pebble room. I want to show you their shapes: spheres, ovoids and flattened ovoids, and cylinders with rounded ends. See what I mean? Pay attention, stop looking at the door by the window.

I read them a passage
in Ellis which ends
"some pebbles are pear-shaped".

— Pear-shaped, echoes Peter,
maybe some pears
are pebble-shaped.

Gemma grabs him:
— look, a beautiful pebble,
with a hole in it.

A hagstone.
The phone rings:
it's Craig.

The visit is on
but first we will go
to the Natural

History Museum.
Why not finish your game
while I take a siesta?

— I've got the advantage.
— Count your pawns,
but don't count your chickens.

16.

"Rose-red city
half as old as time",
I remember its name

and finish the crossword
then go to the garden
where they are busy

on the swing
and trampoline.
Time for the dinosaurs.

Driving along
I ask them to tell me
what they like doing.

— I love dressing up and performing. Sometimes I speak my own poems but I don't write them down. I love putting on my mother's lipstick and eye shadow, but it makes her cross.

— I collect postcards and doing card tricks and stuff like that, which I practise on Gemma when we Skype. I don't collect pebbles.

— Tell you what, shall we go looking for pebbles, one day? I want you to see places like Chesil Beach and Dungeness and the Crumbles near Eastbourne. Crumbles. Crumbles.

— Yes, let's do that.

— The Crumbles is a lovely name, says Peter; is it called that because the rocks crumbled a long time ago?

— Sounds plausible. Raise a glass to Clarence Ellis, and toast him. When you clink glasses, it makes a lovely ringing noise that stays inside your ears for a long time.

— My other grandfather has a ringing noise inside his head all the time, says Gemma. He says he's used to it.

— I'm sorry he has this miserable affliction, it's called tinnitus. I hope I don't get it.

17.

In the museum,
we have a good look
at the dinosaurs,

and the insects,
and the butterflies
with their pinned-back wings.

— Time to go, before the traffic builds up.

We drive past the beach
and boardwalk at Venice,
for Gemma to see,

arrive at the studio
a few minutes late.
Sorry I say,

as Craig approaches,
waving and smiling.
No problem.

Never one
to waste time,
Craig plunges in.

— You can use wood and other materials for lithography and you can do drawings on what is called
transfer paper but I like stone best. I draw directly
on the stone with special greasy wax crayons —
not the pastels some painters use when drawing on
paper, which they mount on aluminium, because it
strengthens the paper. You will have to keep still for
a few minutes while I draw you on the stone which
my colleague Piotr is preparing right now.

We watch Piotr,
a silent man
with a sad

and lonely smile,
cleaning and polishing
the stone to remove

traces of Craig's
previous drawing, to ensure
the surface is level.

— Aren't you the lucky ones to be in a picture?

— No, I'm the lucky one to have beautiful models.

— Grandpa sent me a big box of pastel crayons for my birthday. I love using them. I draw singers and dancers.

— He sent me crayons too, they were from the Prado Museum shop in Madrid, says Peter. I drew my favourite basketball player and then I tried to copy the postcard of a painting he sent with the crayons, a sad dog.

— Ah, it's a famous and beautiful painting by Goya. I love that museum, the works of Goya and Velasquez and Ribera and Zurbaran. Goya was one of the first artists to do lithography, about two hundred years ago. Get grandpa to Google the work of Goya and Henri Toulouse-Lautrec: check out Lautrec's wonderful lithographs of the dancer Loïe Fuller, printed with different colour inks and then hand-coloured. Dunstan, my friend, brush up your Art Nouveau. The stone is ready.

18.

— "Don't move. It will only take a few minutes".

— I'm impressed. What do you think, children?

— It looks like me.

— I wish I could do that, says Peter.

— Watch what happens next.

Piotr the printer begins fixing the image. He speaks for the first time, explaining that he has to use a gum Arabic solution. Because grease and water greatly dislike each other, the image attracts the oily ink but repels water; when the surface is moistened and inked, the ink only adheres to the greasy drawing and not to the rest of the stone, which remains clear so that only the drawn image is transferred to paper.

Craig and Piotr carry the stone over to the printing press where they place it gently into the press bed. The lithography paper has been prepared, and the printer dampens the stone evenly with a sponge and immediately pushes and pulls a rubber roller covered in greasy ink across the surface. The paper is placed face down onto the stone surface and runs through the press under pressure. It is then peeled off the surface of the stone, and lo and behold, a print.

Five copies are printed. Craig takes them one by one to his drawing table and says he will add colour to each print separately. He swiftly and carefully hand-colours the five prints with his crayons; each is slightly different from the others, and therefore unique. Then he numbers the prints: one for Gemma, one for Peter, one for Dunstan, one for Piotr, and one for himself.

— Now you have to wipe the drawing off the stone to make it ready again, says Peter.

— That's right, that's the way stone lithography works. It doesn't matter if the drawing is lost. It lives on in these five copies. The stone is where Hermes lives, the Greek god who is a courier or postman. He brings messages to artists from Apollo and Dionysus, the Gods of art.

— They may be Gods but they're not in the Bible. Grandpa showed us your lithographs of Moses, Jacob and David in his house.

— And the one of him with pebbles in his mouth, says Peter.

— Ah yes, the God of Moses, Jacob and David (and Dunstan?) is very different from the Greek gods. He is unique, indivisible and invisible.

I reflect on Craig's remark about the lost drawing. The stone contains the memory trace of ghost images, the drawings done on its surface over many years. There are hints of fossil from the former life of the stone in the original quarry. Everything connects up.

— Many thanks, Craig, for this lesson. Not only did we not pay you, you paid us with a gift!

— Thank you, say Gemma and Peter.

— It's been my pleasure.

— Time to head back. Thanks again for the prints. Thank you, Piotr, for your work.

— Next time, will you draw us while we're standing on one leg? Gemma asks.

— Climbing a pebble, says Peter.

19.

The moment has arrived. I give Gemma the key to the pebble room. We go in. Facing us is the door in the wall which, when you look up from the garden, goes nowhere. And yet it has to lead somewhere.

I lean gently on the door. The children say nothing but their eyes widen and widen and their pulses race and race and their hearts beat faster and faster and it seems as though they are already in another world.

PART TWO:
PEDRATERRA

Two men were standing in the hall when Dunstan, Peter and Gemma arrived in Pedraterra. They were wearing smart clothes, abstractly patterned identical suits, resembling cross-sections of beautiful pebbles, thought Dunstan. Gilbert and George sprang to his mind. He made a mental note to tell the children about the two artists. The visitors greeted them in English and in return the men bowed. They started talking in their language. Dunstan said it sounded more like Italian or Spanish than those impossible languages Hungarian and Basque because he recognised one or two words, or thought he did: maybe the sound was the same and the meaning was different. Peter said the words sounded like pebbles dropping into water. Dunstan smiled at the references to pebbles and Gemma smiled at his smile, understanding her grandfather's pleasure. The men gestured to the visitors to wait and one of them left the room, returning with a woman who merely smiled when Dunstan said hello. She was wearing a long dress, its pattern a slightly more colourful version of pebble-style than the men's pattern. Dunstan was beginning to wonder if everything in this place was made of stone, or looked like stone. It was as if he had never left his pebble room.

The woman was younger than Dunstan but older than his own children. Her eyes sparkled like polished pebble jewels, her skin was white as alabaster and for a brief moment Dunstan thought she was from another world, forgetting that this was where he told the children they were going. It was as if Peter had conjured her up in one of his magic tricks. Strangely enough, she didn't seem surprised to see them. She was holding three gadgets, three small computers, each attached to a string threaded with small pebbles. She put them round the necks of the visitors, adjusted one of the settings to "English" and pressed a button on her own gadget:

— Welcome to Pedraterra, the City State of Pedraterra. I am responsible for tours of the city. You are our first tourists, so everything is free. You are participating in a trial run, an experiment. The microphone on my computer picked up your conversation and the computer language app recognised which language you were speaking. It makes an immediate translation into our language, just as yours is set to translate what we say into your language. All three of you have slightly different accents, so you come from different countries, or different parts of the same country.

— Thank you, I'm Dunstan; these are my grand-children, Peter and Gemma.

— Come with me, said the gadget woman.

She took the visitors to a simple stone building and explained that this was the office where Pedraterra logistics were organised. Pedraterra, she said, is a prosperous city, a city-state, with an old centre and suburbs all round, and beyond them a network of villages. It has a policy, newly elaborated, to treat eventual visitors as paying guests, with emphasis on the word *guests* so that they would go home and feel good about their time here. Dunstan and the children would be allowed to stay for one day, at the expense of Pedraterra, provided they behaved well and watched their words. An experiment, the woman had said, a trial run. Dunstan was on the alert.

The woman said goodbye to her colleagues and took the visitors to an adjoining room. Explaining to them that she was in charge of tours for residents, she asked an unsmiling man at the desk for three loan agreements and, after signing and getting the three visitors to countersign the forms, said that the formal proceedings were over and their tour could begin.

— Thank you. By the way, I want to tell you that your dress is beautiful. I see it has the pattern of an ovoid slate pebble with a quartz vein running through it.

— How did you know that?

— Grandpa is an expert on pebbles, said Peter.

— He has taught us to love pebbles, said Gemma.

— The dress is not unique, said the woman; The Place of Clothes sells patterned dresses and pullovers.

— The Place of Clothes? said Gemma.

— You mean, a shop? said Dunstan.

— Yes, everything in Pedraterra is called "Place of..." But remember, as our first visitors from outside, you are our guests, you don't have to pay. With your love of pebbles, you will feel at home. Next door to the Place of Clothes is a museum, what we call the Place of Museum, with shelves of pebbles and related exhibits.

— Sounds like Grandpa's pebble room in Los Angeles, said Peter. We should call his room the Place of Pebbles.

— Or the Palace of Pebbles, said Gemma.

Peter and Gemma and Dunstan laughed. Slightly frowning, the woman looked at Dunstan, her sparkling eyes asking the question: why are you all laughing? At least she was not unsmiling, not stony faced like the man in the office. Dunstan registered the sparkling eyes in a part of his mind that had not been used in recent years.

— We're laughing because in my house there is a room which, as Peter says, is my own Place of Pebbles. Inside the room there is a door which from outside the house appears to lead nowhere. When we opened it a few minutes ago (although it seems like hours, but space affects time, a mental jet-lag), it opened onto a tunnel which we descended like a snake in a drain and arrived in this city which you tell us has a proper museum of pebbles, certainly much larger than mine. The world is strange, and coincidence even stranger. By the way, what is your name?

— Petra Sandstone.

— Your first name means stone. It's also the name of a city in Jordan, famous because a scholar priest wrote a poem called 'Petra', which ends: "A rose-red city half as old as time". I visited it during my years as a travel agent. It occurs to me that you, like me, are a kind of travel agent, a tour operator. By the way, my name and the children's too are associated with stone.

— Yes. You will find out soon enough that everybody's name in Pedraterra has to do with stones or rocks or pebbles. But that's enough about names for the time being. You must go on a special tour of the city. There are twenty-six Places for you to visit, including the Place of Clothes: one place for each letter of your alphabet. It would be best to see a few Places properly rather than all of them in a rush. We'll send you a reminder message on your computers an hour before it's time to return, in preparation for departure.

While the grownups were talking, the children slipped away. Five minutes later, there was a ringing sound, like a bee buzzing, on Peter's computer, which alerted him to a voice message.

— I know where you are. I'm just checking that you're okay.

— We're fine. We'll see you later. I'll look after Gemma, he spoke into the computer.

— Yes, we're fine. I don't need looking after.

Dunstan looked at Petra. Petra looked at Dunstan. He smiled but he was nervous and his smile could not disguise his anxiety. He put his hand on hers. She was startled but not displeased. She almost smiled at him but then re-set her face. Stones, he thought, can't do that.

— Grandpa knew where we were. That's spooky. I'd like a dress with the same pattern as Petra's.

— Yes, spooky. I'd like a pullover. Let's look for the Place of Clothes.

They were on the junction of Eben Street and Ciotollo Street but which way was the Place of Clothes? Gemma said Peter should ask someone but he was too shy. Suddenly he had an idea: he pressed a button on his gadget labelled Pedraterra Internet, which was unique to the city. There he spoke into the gadget, which operated by voice recognition and eye-tracking the words, "map of Pedraterra". When that came up, he told the mini-computer that they were on Ciotollo Street, how do you get to the Place of Clothes and the Place of Museum next door? The information came up immediately, like the satnav in grandpa's car, and they turned left onto Ciotollo Street.

CLOTHES

Here was where people bought clothes in Pedraterra. An indoor market, with everything ranged on stone shelves or hanging in stone compartments: underwear and overwear, shoes and sandals, overcoats and raincoats, skirts and trousers, shirts and blouses, socks and tights, underpants and knickers, suits for men and women, cardigans and waistcoats, dresses short and long, all items ranging from casual to smart, from cheap to expensive, but, as the children already knew, they would not have to pay a single Rai, the local currency. Gemma asked a woman in the dress department if she would show them the range.

— Ah yes, you are our visitors. The whole city knows about you!

Gemma and Peter heard the buzzing tone on the woman's computer. They looked at each other. The woman told them that Dunstan wanted to be absolutely sure they were fine, and that Petra had told him they were, and he would not trouble them again.

— Grandpa should relax.

— Petra will calm him down, said Peter, I think he likes her.

— And she likes him.

At that very moment, Dunstan was wondering why Petra had started frowning again. He asked her, via the computer, if anything was wrong. She replied that she was fine but that she was thinking hard about the situation (and she always frowned when thinking) because, as she had already explained, they were the first visitors to Pedraterra. Dunstan had a feeling she was hiding something from him. Now, she said, she needed a cup of strong coffee or black tea. They could go to the nearby Teahouse Kevir-Karkotsel for tea or Café Eben-Hijar for coffee. These were small branches of the Place of Food and Drink, which was the main restaurant, and served many varieties of tea and coffee. Grandpa told Petra that this was a nice problem and that she should make the decision.

They sat drinking coffee for a while but it would soon be time for him to set off, even though he felt like staying with Petra. She could not go with him everywhere because she must work, but she would join him at one or two places. He asked her if Pedra-terra was self-sufficient in food. She replied that they had no way of importing goods. It was time for Pedraterra to open up.

— Does it make any difference if everybody knows about us and what we are doing? Gemma whispered. All the same…

— … It's a bit weird. Still, we're not doing anything wrong, are we? If we were, they'd deport us rather than put us in prison.

While Gemma was looking for the dress which had the same pattern as Petra's, they relaxed and forgot all about the revelation that the whole city knew about them. Finally, with Peter's help, Gemma found a stand with the dress in different sizes. Before she could make a move, the woman looked her up and down, said a size, and took the dress down from the stand. Gemma went into a cubicle to put it on, came out and looked at herself in a full-length mirror. It fitted perfectly of course. She twirled around like a dancer, vaulted like a gymnast, performed a cartwheel and then went back to the cubicle and changed back into the clothes she came in.

— When I'm wearing it, I look like a large pebble. A human pebble. A girl pebble. Gemma Pebble Gebel, G. P. Gebel, W. H. Auden.

— I'd like a pullover, Peter said to the saleswoman. Peter Pebble Kamen, P. P. Kamen. A boy pebble. Grandpa is Dunstan Pebble Gebel. D. P. Gebel. It's like living on Brighton beach.

The woman, who seemed perplexed by the use of initials, explained that the pullovers were on another floor. On the way she explained that Peter and Gemma didn't have to carry the clothes with them during their visit. All packages would be delivered to the exit of Pedraterra, awaiting their departure. She found the pullover salesman, who was wearing a pebble-patterned cardigan over a pebbly tee-shirt.

— He will look after you. Give me your new dress to wrap up.

Before returning to the dress department, the woman told the pullover salesman that the children were two of the three visitors to Pedraterra, but she had forgotten that he already knew about their visit, which reminded the pair about the weirdness of a city where everybody seems to know everything or at least everything about the visitors. They were not surprised that he already knew which pattern Gemma had chosen, the ovoid slate pebble with a quartz vein running through it, and had already placed on the stone table pullovers with the same pattern, picking up one of them after correctly assessing Peter's size at a glance. Peter, however, knew what he wanted, and it wasn't Gemma's chosen pattern. He picked up an unpolished purple jasper pebble pullover and a black and white igneous gabbro pebble pullover and tried them both on. Gemma asked him to try on the one with her and Petra's pattern which he did, to please her and to keep her quiet.

— Go on, have the same pattern as me.

— Maybe not. I'm a different person; I should have a different pattern.

He looked at all three pullovers again before finally choosing the purple pullover pebble. Like his grandfather, he repeated the words, rolling them round his mouth like pebbles: purple pullover pebble.

— I've got an idea, let's get grandpa a present. What do you think he would like?

— How about a tee-shirt?

— Good *ideeea*, said Gemma, pronouncing the word like Peter sometimes did.

Peter smiled. He knew that Gemma was teasing him. It was a kind of compliment. They asked the pullover man where to find the tee-shirt department.

It was through a door, to the left. He said that he also looked after that department and showed them the range. Gemma told the man that Dunstan was about the same size as him, but he already knew. They both pointed to a tee-shirt and asked the man the name of the pattern; grandpa would not have needed to ask. He knew everything about pebbles.

— Red-brown Carnelian pebble.

— That's lovely, just right for grandpa, said Gemma.

— I agree, we'll have that one; thank you.

— Everything will be waiting for you at the exit.

Now it was time to walk down the street to their next Place.

MUSEUM

They entered the Place of Museum, a museum of stones, and saw a sign with directions to different departments on several floors. One section of the stone department was "Pebbles", so they decided to take a look. The guard on duty welcomed them by name. They spent about ten minutes there, recognised some pebbles and then left. Enough was as good as a feast and they were feeling guilty for running off and making Dunstan feel anxious.

— He'll be all right, said Peter.

— Yes. He knows what we are doing.

— But only while he's with Petra. When he goes on his tour he won't know what to do on the computer, unless the techies supplied him with a "parent's button". People can keep tabs on us, but we can't keep tabs on them.

— I don't want to know what he's doing.

— Maybe he's kissing her.

— He's not from this country.

— So what?

— Maybe they don't like visitors to be too friendly. They might think the visitors want to take somebody back with them when they leave.

— Or the visitors might want to stay.

— Grandpa wouldn't send us back on our own!

— Or go back on his own!

— I'm hungry. And thirsty.

— Me too. If we don't find somewhere within the next few minutes, we can consult the computer again.

— Let's do it now.

Up came the "Place of Food and Drink", which they found after zigging and zagging through small streets.

FOOD and DRINK

Gemma and Peter arrived at the Place of Food and Drink. What meal was it, not that it mattered? Lunch probably. Their sense of time was all over the place (or the Place), partly because they were still jet-lagged from their long flights to Los Angeles, partly from what Dunstan would have called the mental jetlag caused by moving to another world, another country, where things were different and done dif-ferently, and therefore experienced differently.

—Welcome, said a young man and young woman who were surely twins.

Her trouser suit and his shirt and kilt were identical in pattern: polished and stained agate pebble, with mauve and black and different shades of brown, elegant and understated.

— Thank you, said the children explaining that they were hungry and thirsty.

— Well, said the woman, before we show you what is on offer, you must have some water, flavoured with lime.

— The drink reminds me of limestone.

— Why do you say that?

Peter kept quiet. The answer was obvious.

— Our grandfather told us about limestone and lithography, said Gemma.

— I'm glad you feel a personal connection with the Place of Food and Drink. Your drink will come in a limestone jug and limestone bowls, which we bring out for important customers, said the man as the woman went off to fetch the drink and the menu.

— Thank you, said Peter, when the waitress returned.

— It's delicious.

While they were drinking a second bowlful of lime water, the waitress put two menus on the table and the waiter spoke.

— We had heard that you were visiting our city, so we prepared a special meal for you. If you don't finish it, you can take the leftovers back with you at the end of your trip.

First Course
Stone Soup

Second Course
Fish Balls
Hard Boiled Eggs with optional mayo
Chips
Salad

<u>Third Course</u>

Rock

Ice cream

> The children looked at each other, their
> mouths watering.

— Sounds great, said Peter.

— Thank you, said Gemma.

— Our pleasure. Why don't you sit at the outside table by the door? The food will be with you soon.

People were walking along the street, which had no cars, like half the streets in the city. While they were waiting for their food, they looked up Alphabet Tour of Pedraterra on their computers and found the full list of Twenty-Six Places. Having been to Clothes and Museum and now the double Place (Food and Drink), they still had twenty-two more to choose from. Peter knew that grandpa had tried to visit all the mainland states of the USA on one visit and almost succeeded but ran out of time before he could go to West Virginia! They discussed possible tour routes and watched Pedraterra people going about their business. Many of the passers-by — all wearing pebble-inspired clothing — looked closely at them and then spoke into the computers they had round their necks. Everyone, from grandparents to babies, was wearing a pebble-patterned outfit and speaking the language which Peter and Gemma couldn't understand. At one point, Peter said something to Gemma, and a woman looked startled and slowed down for a moment.

— Hello.

The woman was about to say something but thought better of it and walked faster before turning into a side street.

— Maybe she's frightened, continued Gemma.

— Of us? Or of something else.

— Those clothes, do they never wear non-pebble clothes?

— No wonder Pedraterra is reached through a door in a pebble room. I hope grandpa is well.

— Of course, he is. If we are, he is.

The first course arrived. In bowls made of beautiful sunstone, with the word Pedraterra Place of Food and Drink emblazoned inside, just under the rim. But that wasn't why the dish was called stone soup. Like two people singing a duet in an opera, the twin waiters explained together that stone soup does not have an identifiable recipe but is different every time it is served, as in an old story all Pedraterra children are taught. Unlike the other dishes whose ingredients are delivered by suppliers, stone soup ingredients are brought by the people who work in the restaurant, and sometimes even by regular customers: vegetables of all shapes and colours, pieces of fish, herbs strong and mild, fruit, cheese, rye bread (and of course stone-ground bread) and other grains, anything and everything. Quite often the ingredients include leftovers, just before they would have to be thrown away. Pedraterra people hate waste. For stone soup, all the bits and pieces are chopped up and thrown in a large sunstone saucepan on a low flame and prepared with olive oil which was so freshly pressed in the backyard of the restaurant that the olive stones were still on a table waiting to be recycled.

— Delicious, said Gemma.

— Fabulous.

— There are so many flavours all mixed up.

— Hmm, I detect lemon, coriander, ginger, blue cheese, onions.

— Liar. There's carrots and olives.

— Glad you like it, said the twins, looking up from their computers. What are you going to visit after the meal?

— We thought we might take the tube, said Peter, what you call the Place of Tube, to the other side of the city.

— It's also called the Place of Names, you'll see why later, said one of the twins, who looked very anxious because the first twin had suddenly vanished and, like Laurel and Hardy, they were accustomed to doing everything together.

— One street has three Places, doesn't it? said Gemma.

— Yes, replied Peter, the Place of Quiz, the Place of Rest and the Place of Karaoke. That will save time.

— And so will the tube, since it doubles as the Place of Names.

There was enough soup for second helpings but Peter decided not to have any more because there was so much food to follow. Gemma asked for a tiny portion. After she had finished, the twins – the missing one had returned — said there were at least four more bowlfuls of soup to take back to Los Angeles and heat up or freeze.

— We'll seal the soup in a large sunstone bowl and any other leftovers in additional bowls which you can keep as a souvenir. They'll be waiting for you at the exit, together with the clothes and anything else you pick up during your visit.

The second course arrived: as the menu stated, there were balls of chopped fish, served up in a beautiful soapstone bowl and shaped like very large chalcedony pebbles; another bowl with hard-boiled eggs: such a shame that Peter and Gemma would have to peel off the beautiful shells painted to look like ovoid pebbles of red serpentine; a third bowl with chips which looked like cylindrical pebbles; and salad chopped up and rounded to look like pebble-dash.

The fish balls reminded Peter and Gemma of their grandmother's chopped fish balls, but the Pedraterra version was sweeter. The hard-boiled eggs were *perfect*: the texture as it should be: the white firm, the yolk slightly softer but not runny. As for the chips: brilliant! And the salad, they agreed, tasted great. But they could not finish the meal, not if they were going to leave any room for pudding.

The ice cream came shaped like seashells and irregular shaped stones. As for the sticks of rock, they looked just like Brighton Rock, except that the word Pedraterra was printed in green inside the white sugary confection. Peter and Gemma only had room for ice-cream and broke off two small pieces of rock to suck like sweets. They were full up, chock-a-block, stuffed. Before leaving, they went onto their computers and read about Pedraterra, including the latest news bulletin. By now, they were not entirely surprised to find a paragraph about themselves at the end of the bulletin. As they left, they saw a sign to the toilets, which reminded them they wanted to go. When they came out, Peter and Gemma went over to the twin waiters:

— Grandpa ought to have a new bath and toilet in his house, made of marble just like here!

— Very funny, said the twins without laughing. We will wrap up the leftovers, including soup, for you to collect when you leave. Next time you visit, you may find that our menu is vegan. Our President is taking advice from experts and will make a decision later. Goodbye, we hope you enjoyed your visit to the Place of Food and Drink.

— Yes, I did, said Peter, fantastic food.

— Goodbye, the meal was great.

TUBE and NAMES

It was time to take the cross-town tube, which was a very small system, not like the London underground, which Peter in particular loved because

there was no tube in Dunedin. He read as much as
he could about the London tube, and studied it on
the Internet. Gemma said he knew more about it
than she did, even though she was the one who lived
in London! In Pedraterra there was only one line
and it had three stops: Wealdstone, where they got
on, Stonebridge and Whetstone.

The Place of Tubes, as they were already aware, was
also the Place of Names. They boarded the train
which was about to leave. Instead of advertisements
such as the ones Gemma recalled from the London
Tube, there were names all over the walls and ceiling
of the train carriages, including ones they knew,
some of them very well: Dunstan, Peter, Gemma,
Piotr, Petra, Craig. Taking it in turns, they read the
others out aloud, which were in alphabetical order –
obviously people in Pedraterra liked alphabets:

Adalstienn

Aglauros

Alan

Alana	Hermione	Rochelle
Amber	Jacinta	Saligram
Beryl	Jade	Sienna
Botolf	Jasper	Stanton
Carne	Jawahar	Stoner
Cephas	Jude	Torsten
Coral	Langston	Tremayne
Crystal	Mason	Winfield
Ebenezer	Micah	Winston
Ernestina	Moti	Wystan
Esmeralda	Nilam	Zur
Evan/Even	Pedro	
Flint	Pekka	
Griselda	Penina	— Where did they find all these names? Gemma asked.
Haldor	Petronella	
Hallmar	Petrushka	
Hermes	Pierrepoint	

— Probably on their internet. We must tell Grandpa about them.

— Look at those cameras. What are they for?

— Security, maybe. Here it's possible that everyone knows something about everyone else. Some people must know everything. Or have a password to a database.

— If some people know everything or have access to everything then they are, what was that word grandpa used at the print studio?

— Paranoid.

They did not get off at the first stop on the short line, Stonebridge. They talked about their lunch and the comment by the twins about vegan food and the decision to be taken by the President of Pedraterra. Gemma said they must remember to discuss this with grandpa. Ten minutes after getting on the train, they were at Whetstone. Following their map they took the short walk to the street with the three Places which were next on their list. But before they arrived, they saw the Place of Exercise and decided to take a quick look. They weren't that interested but, since it was there, they popped in for a few minutes....

EXERCISE

In the place of exercise
people try to lose a size
round the bum or tum or waist
— land of plenty – in great haste,
ounces, pounds and even stones
fall away, they hope, while moans,
sniffs and grunts reveal the strain
as they pedal: off again!

QUIZ

The moment they arrived at the Place of Quiz, Gemma and Peter heard the ringing tone, the buzzing bee which always means there is a message on the computer:

— To obtain an English-language explanation about this place and the quizzes, please reply to this message by saying into your computer the word which describes the image on your screen.

— It's an eight-sided building.

— Yes, the Octagon, which is our parliament.

The Place of Quiz was a large room. It was empty but for thirty three round tables at each of which six school children were seated, with lead pencils and lined yellow notepads. They were wearing identical pebble-patterned shirts and blouses and little caps, and appeared to be answering questions. Teachers were telling them not to consult each other or look things up on their computers. Nobody was smiling.

A moment or two later, one of the teachers, who just happened to be wearing the same patterned dress as Petra (the one Gemma chose in the Place of Clothes), and who had a stern look on her face, came over, greeted them politely and handed them pencils, notepads and the Introductory Quiz.

— Why do you have a special place for quizzes? asked Peter.

— We think it's the best way to test the general knowledge of our children. Our homeland prides itself on having a highly educated population, which is necessary, indeed essential, because apart from the staff in the twenty-six Places and suppliers and cleaners and other servants of the city, everybody in Pedraterra works in some branch of high technology, always involving the most advanced computers and other machines. Did you notice, in the streets which have traffic, all our cars are electric? That's the way to do it.

— Mr Punch says "that's the way to do it" when he hits Judy on the head, said Gemma.

— Really? Who is Mr Punch?

Peter described performance art and street theatre and puppets to the teacher.

— How interesting. One of our own puppet shows is about future visitors to Pedraterra and their adventures.

— The future is now the present, said Peter.

— Yes, the story has come to life. Welcome to the Place of Quiz.

At this point, the Pedraterra children looked up. The teacher told them to carry on with the quiz; later they could set their computers so that they could talk to the visitors and vice versa, if they wanted to. She then invited Peter and Gemma to do the Introductory Quiz.

Question One

What is a pebble?

Question Two

How many shapes of pebble are there?

Question Three

What causes the shape?

Question Four

Who is Clarence Ellis?

Peter and Gemma knew the answers to these questions and then got stuck. The other questions were about the history and geography of pebbles, too difficult to answer without the help of Clarence Ellis's book. Grandpa could have done the whole quiz in five minutes. They told the teacher they were tired and would now go to the Place of Rest.

— If that's what you want, feel free to leave. Maybe, when they've finished the quiz, some of the children will join you there or in the Place of Karaoke, depending on their energy level.

REST

The Place of Rest had three large rooms, the quiet room, the talking room and the eating room. Peter and Gemma went to the quiet room, where talking was not permitted. The armchairs were covered with pebble-patterned blankets. The peace and quiet reminded them they were tired. They sat silently for half an hour, and then, hearing the familiar buzz, checked out their computers, finding a new message from the teacher: two of the children would be looking for them soon, not in the Place of Rest but in the Place of Karaoke. She also told them they could get a free drink by entering a code — "smooth stone" – in the drink machine in the talking room, which was where they went next. Sipping their lime juice cordial, they listened to people talking in the Pedraterra language and then walked the few yards to the Place of Karaoke.

KARAOKE

As they entered the Place of Karaoke, Peter and Gemma saw children watching a video on a big screen and listening to the music of a famous song: 'Like a Rolling Stone', but the singer himself could not be heard. Someone in the Karaoke room was singing the words. Two of the children came over to them and, after setting their computers to the language app, introduced themselves. Their names were Ebenezer and Petronella and they had seen Peter and Gemma in the Place of Quiz.

— Do you like being in Pedraterra? Ebenezer asked.

— In some ways, said Peter, politely. It's very different from our home towns.

— Where's your home?

— Ebenezer, you've forgotten, said Petronella, it was on the news and my mother knew even before it was on the news. They've been staying with their grandfather, who lives in the USA.

— Sorry I forgot. Why in some ways? Don't you like everything?

— I'll tell you later.

— OK. Would you like to sing?

— Maybe, said Peter.

— Yes, said Gemma.

— Think of a song. Our leader decided recently we should listen to some songs from outside Pedraterra.

— 'Rock around the Clock', she said.

— We could take it turns to sing solo or all sing together, said Ebenezer.

Peter thought about it for a moment and decided he would like to sing with the others. He definitely did not want to sing solo. Gemma, he knew, would have felt able to do that but even she said no to the solo.

The four of them watched and listened till the end of 'Like a Rolling Stone'. Before any of the other children in the room could get there before him, Ebenezer moved swiftly to the beautiful stone machine and set it to play 'Rock around the Clock' but, before pressing the button, clapped his hands and made an announcement. Everyone looked at the visitors whom they knew about from the news bulletin or various announcements on their computers and clapped. Well, not everyone clapped. Some of the children looked at them stonily. Two tall twins came over and told them they were not welcome in Pedraterra because they were from somewhere else and should go back to their own country. Pedraterra belongs to the natives. This was not pleasant but fortunately many other children were angry and said so. Petronella apologised to the guests and insisted that only a small majority of people in Pedraterra, about fifty two per cent she had heard on the news, were ignorant and prejudiced. She reassured Gemma and Peter that the rest of the people would welcome visitors, the President who was a very moral man was in favour, and the government would be dealing with the problem. Like in Los Angeles probably, Pedraterra people were not all the same, as was obvious from what was happening now. Gemma and Peter looked at each other uneasily. There were discussions at home about people who objected to foreigners. Gemma remembered her parents' reaction while they were watching on television a demonstration which had banners with the words "stick to your own kind": more like "stick to your own unkind", Gemma's mother had said angrily.

Now it was time for 'Rock around the Clock'. The tall twins and some other children, who probably disliked foreign music and foreign visitors equally, left the Place of Karaoke. Those remaining, apart from the four singers, danced. For a few minutes, while they were singing – with the help of the original words on their computer screens, which — on a large screen above the jukebox – had been translated into Pedraterra language — Peter and Gemma managed to forget the unpleasant episode involving the two twins.

The song and dance ended and everyone clapped. Peter and Gemma heard a buzz on their computers and read the message immediately: "You have one hour to return to the exit. If you don't get there in time, you will have to stay here for ever".

— Help, said Gemma, we must leave immediately. We've only been to… how many Places?

— Clothes, Museum, Food, Drink, Tube, Names, Exercise, Quiz, Rest, Karaoke, replied Peter.

— That makes ten. No time to go anywhere else. We can't risk being stuck here forever.

— Yes. We must run to the train and go to the office near the exit. On the way we can read about the other places on the computer.

— I hope we don't have any trouble from prejudiced inhabitants. It's horrible. Thank goodness they are only a small majority.

— They'll only be too pleased to learn we're on our way home.

— Or keep us here in order to be cruel.

They waved goodbye to everyone in the Place of Karaoke and told Ebenezer and Petronella that maybe they would all meet again one day.

— Where, said the two Pedraterra children?

— In Los Angeles of course, replied Peter and Gemma together.

Ebenezer and Petronella smiled warmly – perhaps the first smiles the visitors had seen in Pedraterra — but were silent.

Peter and Gemma left the Place of Karaoke and, holding hands, ran to Whetstone Station. They were relieved that the train arrived within five minutes. They spotted an empty carriage. As soon as they were seated, Peter spoke into his computer the words "Alphabet of Places" so that they could find out what they had missed. When they got back to Los Angeles, they could read about them in detail. And then he remembered that Pedraterra had its own Internet: what if you couldn't obtain Pedraterra information when you were no longer there?

The Alphabet of Places came up on the screens. Peter had a feeling that everybody in Pedraterra was being informed that he had made a request. Part of him didn't mind: after all, there was nothing wrong in being interested in the Alphabet of Places. But part of him was troubled.

THE ALPHABET OF PLACES

(places already visited are in capital letters)

Art	Jokes	Sport
Books	KARAOKE	TUBE
CLOTHES	Law	University
DRINK	MUSEUM	Virtual
EXERCISE	NAMES	Wonder
FOOD	Octagon	X
Games	Palace	Yesterday
Hotel	QUIZ	Zoo
Instruments	REST	

— Just in case we can't get find out about Pedraterra in Los Angeles, let's ask Petra if she can supply
information about the places we didn't visit.

They arrived at Wealdstone and easily found their
way back to the exit.

— I ought to be cross with you for vanishing, said
Grandpa, and I would have been cross if we were in
Los Angeles, but here you are, safe.

— We want to tell you what happened to us at the
Place of Karaoke and lots of other things, said Peter.

— Yes yes, we must tell you.

— But I....

Dunstan was going to say "know" and then thought
better of it when he caught Petra's eye. The children
could be told later about certain aspects of Pedraterra, which had shocked him, although he'd said
nothing openly to Petra. But Gemma and Peter were
smart, and he suspected they had already figured
things out. And they now knew he had a special
button on his computer. His surveillance set-up at
home was his guilty secret.

— Tell me after we've returned. By the way, Petra is coming with us. Nobody else knows.

Peter and Gemma couldn't believe their ears. Or their eyes. Petra smiled – the first full smile they had seen on the face of someone from Pedraterra apart from Ebenezer and Petronella — and with her smooth white alabaster hand she patted the wrinkled back of grandpa's hand with its prominent veins. She told the children via the language app not to forget to pick up the packages of food – including the bowls of soup — and clothes which were waiting for them, beautifully wrapped in pebble patterned paper. Also, they and Dunstan must put their computers on the stone table just before leaving Pedraterra.

— Please, Petra, could you print out for us the information about the places we didn't have time to visit.

— I'll organise shortened versions. Give me your list.

She did not say that she already knew which places and went into the office. Five minutes later, she was back with the information, computer-translated into English of course, which they started reading immediately and very fast — in case they would not be allowed to take the pages with them.

ART

The Place of Art is an educational institution where all techniques are explained. Once a month, an artist comes here to explain a particular method. This month, we have a lithographer: Langston Flint, and an etcher, Tertius Saxby Mason, who will demonstrate the technique known as dry point. Later we will explore pastel painting and water mixable oil paints. There is a room for children to explore their creativity. This month they will be painting stones. The President would also like us to make tiles, stone rather than ceramic. He would like a counterpoint to the typical pebble-dash finish on our houses.

BOOKS

The Place of Books is the main library and bookshop and book museum in Pedraterra. As already announced, we will be supplying print books until the end of the year, at which point they will no longer be available. We will not forbid you to keep your print books. Indeed, it is important to remember the past even as we move into the future.

You must encourage your children to read on screen. Our book of the month is *The Pebbles on the Beach* by Clarence Ellis which will be translated into our language from English, the first book to be translated from any language. This is the favourite book of our visitor to Pedraterra, Dunstan Gebel, who is here for one day with his grandchildren, Peter Kamen and Gemma Gebel. *The Pebbles on the Beach* will be the last print book to be published in Pedraterra. The government is printing extra copies as we are expecting a big demand. When it is published, you will be able to buy copies for yourself and your friends in the bookshop or, if you prefer, borrow the book from the library, although there is likely to be a long waiting list. The Place of Books has a permanent exhibition of the history of printing, including reproductions of work by Jasper Blackburn and James Joseph Mason. In future, however, all reading will be on screens.

GAMES

The Place of Games is one of the biggest Places in Pedraterra. You can play all kinds of games here, whether for grownups or children or the whole family. Among the options are marbles and fivestones and chess. Our two young visitors may want to play chess if they have time to visit this popular Place. Earlier today our other visitor, Dunstan Gebel, challenged Pedraterra tour operator, Petra Sandstone, to a game, which was close-fought before being won by Petra.

HOTEL

We encourage people to sleep at home but sometimes there is a good reason to spend a night at the Place of Residence, widely known as the hotel. Suppliers of goods for the Place of Clothes and the Place of Games, for example, might be too tired to go home, or cleaners who have done a double shift. The hotel has a good restaurant. Among the most popular dishes is stone soup, which is brought here from the Place of Food and Drink.

INSTRUMENTS

All residents of Pedraterra are encouraged to learn music and play an instrument. The Place of Instruments contains a library where you can study the history of music and musical instruments. It also has a concert hall: the programmers specialise in family concerts which feature particular instruments. After the concert the performers hold informal discussions with parents and children. This month the featured instruments are lithophones such as the stone marimba and the steinspiel. Paradoxically, silence is encouraged in the Place of Instruments. Without silence there is no pattern in noise, and pattern is what we must be taught or teach ourselves to discern, if we are to make sense of the screens which are our life.

JOKES

The Place of Jokes is where we learn about jokes and puns and nonsense verse and enjoy ourselves. Some of our residents have been too strict about the nature of study. The government of Pedraterra wants to encourage a balanced diet of serious thought and light-heartedness. Residents are encouraged to contribute to the stock of jokes and puns and to try their hand at writing nonsense poems. Here is a brief selection:

Which bird is stoned? Crow

What is the cry of amazement? Stone me.

Why is this man stony faced? Because he is stony broke.

LAW

The Place of Law is where court cases are heard by a team of judges, sometimes with a jury. The rules concerning who may serve on a jury are quite strict and can be found in appropriate Places. Lapidary statements like "Judge your neighbour like yourself" and "Watchfulness Tempered by Justice" and "Be Prejudiced against Prejudice" are to be found on the door of each courtroom carved into stone by our craftsmen. Crime is becoming rarer and rarer in Pedraterra but non-criminal or civil disputes, arbitration and similar procedures are heard in public. Our visitor Dunstan was brought here by our tour specialist Petra after spending an hour in the zoo.

OCTAGON

The Place of Government is popularly known as the Octagon because of its shape. Here parliament meets when required, under our political system known as "parliamentary governance". The shape of the building reflects our view that there are eight questions for every answer. The official Opposition is supplied with questions from the President and poses the questions to the Government, which chooses two answers and then sends them back to the President for a decision. According to the timetable, the main subject for discussion and resolution is once more that of prejudice, which the government is determined to stamp out, by moral example rather than through the law courts. There was a shameful example today in the Place of Karaoke. A stern eye will be kept on these people. The Octagon is open every day of the year, except President's Day, and citizens of Pedraterra are welcome to visit on a guided tour. The Place of Government has branches of Teahouse Kevir-Karkotsel and Café Eben-Hijar.

PALACE

This building, known as Place of the Father, is next door to the Octagon and linked by a tunnel. The building is shaped like a three-dimensional triangle, a tetrahedron, reflecting our belief in the eternal triangle of people, president and Pedraterra, which was first proposed by the great grandfather of our current president, Winston Pierrepoint the Fourth, whose official residence this is.

SPORT

The Place of Sport is next door to the Place of Exercise, which is for adults only.

This fully equipped indoor sports centre invites grownups and children to participate in many different kinds of activity. They include tossing the stone caber, which takes place in the large playing field at the back of the building. A popular activity for our children is abseiling, taught by Hermione Tremayne. Varieties of gymnastics are overseen by her cousins, Botolf and Cephas. The Tremayne family is legendary in Pedraterra for its physical skills. In Pedraterra it is usual for families, across the generations, to specialise in particular jobs and trades.

UNIVERSITY

The Place of Learning, which is the formal name for the University College of Pedraterra (known popularly as UCP), is a matter of pride for the people of the city. Every subject is taught here. Some are voluntary, some are compulsory, such as civics, geology and mathematics. There are morning classes for student parents with young babies, so that mother and father do not miss out on education. There are seminars for senior citizens and from time to time there is a public lecture. The next one is on "Rock Gardens and Meditation". Retired lecturers are available as counsellors to help students deal with personal issues that they might not feel able to share with their parents. Among the specialists are cognitive therapists, stone advisors, holiday planners. In an age of four dimensional learning and eternal screens, Pedraterra believes strongly in the personal touch.

VIRTUAL

The Place of Virtual Reality is where anyone who has problems with computers, mainly older folk, can find out how the machines work and how to make best use of them and even how to repair them. Here oldsters can improve their awareness of the fourth dimension, the digital world, where our personal being is expanded and deepened, where life on the screen around our neck interacts with our body and mind all the time, even when we are asleep and learning via head attachments, during the hours of the Noctiversity of Pedraterra (ten in the evening till six in the morning). The Place of Virtual Reality houses a research institute which supplies new ideas to the government for the education and leisure of the people.

WONDER

This is the Place of Wonder. Wonderland. Each inhabitant of Pedraterra is invited here on his or her fiftieth birthday to tell a story, either about their own life or in the form of a fable. But, as our visitor Dunstan Gebel said — when he came here after visiting the Place of Animals and the Place of Law — invented stories, fables, often draw on your own life (even if they involve imagining the life you or your parents did *not* live) and stories about your own life involve selection and points of view and in many respects are made up. How lucky composers are, he said. They can say whatever they like in their music without hurting anybody's feelings and nobody will know. The same goes for what he calls abstract expressionist painters, about whom he gave a short talk. Then Dunstan told us about his work as a travel agent and his writing and, above all, his love of pebbles, which should make him feel at home, among us, in Pedraterra.

X

The Place of X is a mark on the ground in the exact centre of Pedraterra. If you could see Pedraterra from the air you would see that it is a circle, with a circular wall around it, built in four different stones and with sectors called North Circular, South Circular, West Circular and East Circular. X marks the spot where we are centred. We belong here, each one of us at the centre of the circle, which is the Pedraterra family. The circle is a favoured motif in our art, and artists are encouraged to explore its possibilities.

YESTERDAY

The Place of Yesterday is a new museum, opened recently by Winston Pierrepoint, the son of our President. Winston junior, who was ten years old on the day of opening, was chosen for this task by his father who made the announcement in a speech which the whole country tuned into and which began: "I have been President for forty years. One of these years I myself will be yesterday. But not for a long time. I will retire on my hundredth birthday. My son Winston is the fifth Winston. He is the future. One day he too will be yesterday. The task of children is to become worthy ancestors when that time comes". The museum documents the digital past of everybody in Pedraterra: a complete record of all aspects of their life. Some of the material, especially the life of the President, is confidential for security reasons.

ZOO

The Place of Animals is very popular with the children of Pedraterra. Here they come with their parents to talk to Haldor the Mynah bird who repeats back what you say to him: "Show us your pullover" or "I'm stony broke". Here, slugs and ants can be observed, and beekeeping is taught. Here the extinct roc is brought back to life thanks to a brand new interactive four-dimensional mul-tisensorial programme housed in a hall upstairs called the Roxydrome, to honour the late mother of our President, Roxana Pierrepoint. Every letter of the alphabet is represented: alligator, baboon, cow, donkey, emu, fox, giraffe, human, ibis, jackal, kangaroo, lemming, mouse, newt, ostrich, possum, quail, reindeer, skunk, tiger, umbrella bird, vulture, warthog, x-ray tetra, yak, zebra. Human? Yes, but we are not cruel. We do not keep a human in a cage permanently. We ask for volunteers to serve as the human specimen for one day (or more if they want) during opening hours. This teaches us our place in the alphabet of species. Today's human has been Aglauros Saligram who was joined for one hour by Dunstan Gebel. Dunstan was recognised and approached politely by a keeper. The keeper asked him to participate in the interests of science and morality. Some volunteers are obliged to participate because their behaviour needs improving.

The children finished reading and looked at each other. They had nothing to say but the weary and perplexed expression on their faces told a story: time to go home. Petra placed her computer on the stone table next to the other three. Apparently unobserved, she pressed a button in the wall and followed Dunstan and the children (who were clutching their packages) to the opening which led back to his pebble room, his Place of Pebbles.

PART THREE:
LOS ANGELES

1.

Back in the pebble room, I place the food packages on the floor and give the children and Petra a hug. Life is a dream.

— All these pebbles! Give me a break. I'm sick and tired of stone.

We laugh and then fall silent, as we register with amazement that Petra is speaking English, correct English too. How long has she been hostile to stone?

— Sorry I had to pretend in Pedraterra that I didn't know English. Perhaps Dunstan would make a pot of tea.

— Yes, and we'll have it in the sitting room.

I bring in the tea and apple cake made according to the recipe of my grandmother.

— It's time to tell you what is going on. The President has convened a top-secret foreign policy study group. Thanks to a phenomenally expensive technological fix (magic if you like), his cyber-master managed to access your internet and delegated to his most trusted deputy the task of profiling, finding and persuading people to support Pedraterra. Although we are an advanced country in some ways, the President wants to keep up with the latest developments in industry, travel and science. He naively hopes that Pedraterra will become a respected member of the family of nations, and even teach them a thing or two.

— Family, that's a joke.

— You know what I mean. The deputy found a couple called Tara and Dustin Cornelian. The Cornelians and their friends were enlisted to teach English online to a group of Pedraterrans, including myself, who might one day visit the Anglosphere and report back on societies such as the USA, the UK and New Zealand. We had permission to work half time at our day jobs, while studying with these people, who made recordings for us. It turns out that the Cornelians have a deep grudge against their native country, which took the wrong path when it executed Charles the First. They are members of a secret faction of the English National Party, known as the Saxon Angle. They hate Europe (as well as Scotland, Ireland and Wales) and want the UK to join the United States. The deputy failed to discover this embarrassing profile and has lost his job. My visit is not officially sanctioned and they are turning a blind eye. I suppose I am a kind of diplomat, an honorary consul. The President does not know that I intend never to return. Their surveillance only works in Pedraterra.

— It must be clear by now that I have mixed feelings about my native land. I am a patriot. I've read about the British concept of loyal opposition and love it. In my mind I'm a leader of the opposition. I want to rid Pedraterra of its crazy surveillance and its obsession with stone and build upon its unexpectedly progressive policies concerning climate change, which I will explain to you later. I have to be very discreet. I feel like a double agent. The President is not completely stupid. I suppose he and I are using each other. I hope you won't hold this new information against me. I would do anything for you. But if you feel compromised, I will go back to Pedraterra.

— Don't be ridiculous. Children, show Petra round the house, I'll go and see what's in the fridge. Dinner time soon.

I struggle to make sense of these revelations. Is she really in love with me? Or is she a chimera, a character in a children's story? Her words have the ring of truth. In any case, what about my camera on the roof and its link to my smart phone? That makes me a low-level spy. Perhaps we are all double agents. I open the fridge door and remember the food packages, still in the pebble room, which I fetch: soup, fish balls, eggs, salad and rock – enough for four. Only the soup needs heating up. Perfect, I'm too tired to cook.

The clothes and the food bowls – sunstone and soapstone — are the only material souvenirs of our visit. One day, Peter and Gemma will tell their children about Pedraterra. After my death, Petra will still be around, an elderly lady with more memories than if she was a thousand years old.

— Dinner will be ready in about ten minutes, I shout through the open doors. Just warming up the soup.

2.

We're all tired. It's like jet-lag, on top of the children's earlier jet-lag. Petra is telling them about her online English lessons and how hard she had to concentrate, about the nature of Pedraterra, the president's obsession with stone and how stone is essential to the self-image of the country. She repeats that she is sick and tired of stone. She tells them about the authoritarian government and the President who yearns to be loved and respected by his people but if not, not. He follows with keen interest the United Nations and world politics and he claims that his version of "parliamentary governance", so-called managed democracy, under his family and associates, will catch on and be imitated by other countries. One day, his son will succeed him, and then his grandson. The President issues edicts to counter climate change; veganism will be compulsory, gasoline and diesel forbidden. His is the best of both worlds or so he claims: hyper-elite government pursuing progressive policies. Petra thinks she might become a vegan but not yet.

— I'm so glad Petra's staying, aren't you, Peter?

— Yes, but next week our holiday will be over.

— Gemma and Peter, we will keep in touch: I will see Gemma in London when Dunstan and I visit England and Peter will join us from Dunedin during school holidays. In any case, we will visit New Zealand as soon as possible after that. Dunstan will want to check out the pebbles there, they are part of his extended family, unfortunately! I want to turn his mind in other directions.

— You mean in your direction.

— Watch it, Gemma.

— It must be ten minutes. See if dinner's ready, I'm hungry and you must be too.

As they come into the kitchen, the children's eyes are asking unspoken questions. I smile and tell them that, surprising as it may seem, Petra and I fell in love at first sight and I now realise that our visit to Pedraterra provided her with the opportunity to expedite her quasi-officially sanctioned intention and secret desire: to serve Pedraterra abroad.

— Give me five more minutes. Show Petra the garden, if she's not already there.

— Hi, she says, waving from the swing.

— Grub's up!

— I hate to admit it, says Petra, but Pedraterra food is good, especially the soup. I don't fancy the rock.

— Time for bed, kids.

— I'll help you tidy the kitchen. This is not the moment to have a serious discussion with you about the place of stone in your life, says Petra, looking hard at the bowls, while everyone looks hard at her.

She puts her arm around me. We have decided not to share a room while the children are in Los Angeles. Perhaps that's old-fashioned in this day and age. I have made up a bed for her in the pebble room, but she asks me if I would sleep there instead because it reminds her too much of Pedraterra, which to my ears is a two-edged remark. She kisses me and the children, and goes off to my bedroom, taking with her some books set in Los Angeles which I had chosen for her. Peter and Gemma are over-excited so I relent and usher them into the sitting room because I want to watch the news, but they start telling me about everything they did in Pedraterra. Carried away, they forget that, thanks to technology and the presence of Petra, I already knew. I pretend to be ignorant and listen to their graphic accounts.

— I'm tired.

— So am I.

— Me too, I'm absolutely shattered. Tomorrow we must think about what you are going to do for the rest of your stay, and what will interest Petra too. Goodnight, I'll be asleep before you, dreaming about taking you to beaches, about climbing a pebble.

3.

— Grandpa thinks a lot about pebbles, doesn't he?

— Yes, says Gemma. And about Petra.

— Petra's not in her room, grandpa.

— She's in the garden. Breakfast is ready. They fetch her from the swing.

— I must check overnight emails, so I'll leave you for a while. When you've had breakfast, enjoy what the garden has to offer. I remember your chess skills from our game in Pedraterra. You should take on Gemma and Peter.

— First, I want to brief myself about the USA and UK and New Zealand on my lap-top and take a look through the Los Angeles novels you gave me by John Fante, Raymond Chandler and James Elroy.

Sipping coffee in my office, I try to banish a dark thought my writerly imagination conjures up: what might happen in the unlikely event that Petra returns to Pedraterra? The regime might turn against her and make an example of the first person ever to leave the country, perhaps putting her on display in the zoo as a "volunteer" for a month or longer. On the other hand, the President might want to show that he can be lenient, in which case he would take into consideration her record of service – she is highly regarded and one senior figure wants or more likely wanted her to be promoted to a senior post. They could use her knowledge, however small, of what the President in his weekly broadcast called the other world. (Petra has told me that the President veers between contempt and envy when contem-plating the world outside Pedraterra).

I trust her, I love her, but a double-agent? Oh, oh, oh. Have I and the children merely (merely!) imagined that she came with us? How did she trick the surveillance, if indeed she did? And if she is a figment of the imagination, maybe I am imagining something else: not only is Petra a dream, she is a dream-within-a-dream. Nonsense! Petra is as real as Peter and Gemma and my goldfish Calderon, whose presence the children have not commented on. What about the bowls? Stone represents the materialisation of spirit, says Jung. The golden bowl must not be broken.

Petra and the grandchildren are my main reason for staying alive. I will deny them the sadness of my death for a long time! There are other reasons too for staying alive: my wider family, my writing, my pebbles. I can't imagine life without any of these.

4.

Although it seems much longer, I've only been away from the computer for a little over twenty-four hours — so there are not all that many emails in the in-box: the online *Guardian* and *New York Times* and a bulletin from *The Travel Writer*, all of which I leave for now, one or two messages from friends and colleagues, and two from my own children, Peter's mother and Gemma's father, which I will reply to first, confirming flight times, and without mentioning Pedraterra.

— Dunstan, I have mixed feelings about keeping Pedraterra things, the bowls, and the dress I'm wearing and the underwear which you haven't seen yet. All clothes have Pedraterra labels. And the bowls too are inscribed with the word, not to mention the rock.

She smiles. I can't believe it, here am I in my computer chair facing Petra installed in the armchair where I do my print reading before going to bed. I am not imagining her.

— I understand your mixed feelings. The Pedraterra rock reminds me of a song by Burl Ives, 'Big Rock Candy Mountain'. Here it is on YouTube, listen.

The lyrics are harsher and stranger than I recalled. Negative feelings about Pedraterra are appropriate and understandable. But I want to make a case for keeping material proof of the visit, forensic evidence that, if or when it becomes necessary, will stand up in the court of sceptical opinion (the parents of the children will be a test case), evidence that will ground the dimensions of memories, feelings and knowledge.

— You make a good case, dear Dunstan. What is in my best interests, your best interests, the children's best interests and, in the long term, the best interests of Pedraterra? My head tells me we must preserve the material evidence that the country exists: rock, bowl, and the clothes even after the children have grown out of them. My heart says break the bowls, my head says save them. Memory is not enough.

— Thank you, dear Petra. I'm proud of you, if I may put it that way. I won't ask to inspect the pieces of evidence I haven't yet seen. I am a patient man, pebble experts have no choice. Now it's time to look forward, make a plan the week ahead. When they leave, we'll miss them and we'll have a honeymoon. But we must begin with a trip to the nearest shopping centre, to buy whatever clothes and toiletries you need. At least I had a spare toothbrush for you last night.

She puts her hand on my chest, kisses me and takes a deep breath, a princess breathing life into an old statue.

— I might once have objected to your "putting it that way". But I have been thinking about you and your pebble room and what it tells me about your cast of mind and I am going to ask you to think hard about what I am going to say. I hope, in turn, that I shall be even prouder of you than I am already, if I in turn may put it that way.

— Oh dear, this sounds like a tough call. You are softening me up. Before you explain, I've just realised that the email from the *Travel Writer* is a personal message from the editor, a friend of mine. Here's twenty dollars. Why don't you ask the children to go to the shops and get the latest *New York Review of Books*, a box of caramels for us, and treats for themselves. That will buy us time to talk uninterrupted. It's fifteen minutes dawdle to Westwood Boulevard – left outside the door then right — and doubtless a little longer coming back.

5.

— The children have gone. I think they were pleased to get out of the house and equally pleased to do something for us. Peter is still wearing his purple pullover. Gemma said she would wear her dress on another occasion. As soon as we've had our conversation, we'll go shopping for clothes.

— Yes of course, darling. Now read this email from my friend and comrade, Musa Yeshim-Tashuh.

Dear Dunstan,

I hope you are well. I am writing to tell you that you have been awarded the first Silver Cord *Travel Writer* award for excellence, which will be given every fiveyears. The committee is independent of the sponsors and not all are in the travel business. I want you to know, Dunstan, that your "combination of learning, humour, observation, educated concern for climate issues and, not least, prose style" (in the words of the citation), combine to make you talked about

in professional travel circles far more than
you, with your modesty and self-depreca-
tion, could possibly envisage. In addition,
the latest generation of travel writers and
indeed travellers in general admire you
for visiting every place you write about,
rather than relying on the internet or other
secondary sources. You are considered a
role model by many writers.

 If you accept, you will be presented with
the Silver Cord and a cheque for thirty
thousand pounds, courtesy of our green-
leaning sponsors, all signed up to the ethical
charter you helped draft a few years ago.
There is one condition: you must write a
book. If it involves travel (ha ha), you will
receive full expenses. I note a loophole. It
does not say travel book, it says: book. No
reason why you shouldn't write a novel, my
dear. Only saying.

Love and congratulations, your friend

Musa Yeshim-Tashuh
Editor, *Travel Writer*

— Utterly amazing. What will you do?

— I'm overwhelmed. This is the first professional recognition of my work. I want you to be "even prouder of me" than you are, but I know this is going to involve a difficult conversation about stone, since you specifically mentioned the pebble room. As to what I will do, what sort of book I will write, it's very tempting to write a novel. This will surely involve travel, so I'd get the best of both worlds. I'll make tea.

6.

We drink our tea in silence. Petra shifts from ham to ham in the armchair. I cough and scratch and wait.

— You are in danger of being petrified, Dunstan: you're frozen in your fear, frozen in your stone. I concede immediately that without your pebble obsession, your pebble world, you would not have come to Pedraterra, at least not literally. In a sense, you were already there. Pedraterra projected the world of your mind into three dimensions, only carried to an extreme. Think what stone does to our heads in Pedraterra, even though you only stayed for a day. It is an objective correlative, a cast of mind, our minds are cast stone. I admit that not everyone has been spellbound. As in every country, there are intelligent people and stupid people, good people and bad people, susceptible people and potentially rebellious people. Not all have been brainwashed and some never will be. However, a serious rebellion will be quashed unmercifully. You, a democrat, a sweetheart, a child at heart, a man of gifts, are the most benign version of the stone-touched human imaginable, but you are straitjacketed.

— Dunstan, try to understand, you must, for the sake of your sanity, not to mention your legacy, begin making a shift from this monolithic landscape. Let stone be your servant, not your master, lest a great prince remain incarcerated. Release him in your book. You told me in Pedraterra about your time in the pebble room with the children. Let that be the end rather than the beginning of a phase of your life, lest it strike you deader than a great reckoning in a little room. But you must not make this shift for love of me, you must do it because you want to, because you are a king not of stone but of flesh and blood.

She puts her finger to her lips, and undresses. I too undress. In silence, we make love gently but fast, not wanting to be discovered by the children when they arrive home from the shopping trip. Petra stands up.

— I'll take a shower and borrow some of your clothes until we go shopping, even if I look bizarre for an hour or two.

— Ah, I have a dress and underwear I wore for a carnival party at my friend Craig's house where everyone had to cross dress as movie characters or painted portraits. We'll tell the children that you did not want to go out in your Pedraterra dress and in any case, you needed to shower and no one wants to get back into dirty clothes. Hurry, we'll have time to continue our conversation before Peter and Gemma get back.

Before leaving the room, she kisses me on the head, which is whirling like a dervish. I take a few deep breaths and reread Musa's email. A novel. I need a subject. Is Petra over-reacting to the extremes of Pedraterra or does she have a point? Am I nothing but a dry old stick, climbing pebbles, making puns, quoting poems about stone, tolerated by the children for how many more years before they start dating? Is my relationship with their future step-grandmother going to be in creative tension or permanent dis-harmony? Will I kill the stone guest in myself or be killed? *Don Giovanni*! Haven't listened to it for a while. Petra returns in my fancy-dress that is slightly too large. She halts, listening to the music.

We hear the children return. We have no choice but to go shopping and continue in the evening after they've gone to bed. The children smile at her appearance and hardly need to be told the reasons.

They give me the journal and Petra the chocolates. They've already eaten their own treats — there was enough money over to buy a *Dr. Who* DVD.

— When we get back from buying clothes and food for dinner, we'll discuss what we are going to do for the rest of your stay.

— While you're out, we'll play chess or table tennis.

7.

We walk slowly to Westwood Boulevard. I tell Petra the story of Mozart's *Don Giovanni* and then ask her what it was like growing up in Pedraterra. She says this is a painful subject and she would prefer to discuss it on another occasion. I point out houses that once belonged to film stars, such as Peter Lorre.

— Privileged people in Pedraterra, like my family, could watch movies pirated from the outside world. Not everything the President loves is bad, although it's tempting to make the assumption, even morally necessary.

— Let's have tea in my favourite haunt, the Coffee Bean, where I write letters, real letters, to friends who don't have computers. I also correct printed-out proofs there, mainly for my travel writings. I even begin first drafts of books there.

— Maybe Musa's email will inspire you.

After glancing into the entrance of UCLA, we end up in the Coffee Bean. I kiss the waitress Tracy and introduce her to Petra, who looks her up and down and smiles.

We sit there quietly, drinking tea, holding hands, saying nothing. I tell her about Craig and Piotr. Half an hour later, we pay the bill, banter with Tracy (who doubles as a tour guide at the Getty Museum), and push off to the supermarket, Target, next door. Upstairs, in the ladies wear department, Petra swiftly buys a dress, jeans, jumper and cardigan, socks and shoes, and tights and matching bras and panties. These will keep her going for a while. Food shopping is downstairs: we have to top up on staples and buy stuff for dinner.

Back home, we find the children watching *Dr Who*.

— We'll start fixing dinner.

8.

— So, what would you like to do during the remaining days?

— We'd like to visit Craig.

— And Piotr.

— Count me in, says Petra.

— Grandpa, on the way to Craig's the other day, you drove by the beach in Venice so that I could see it, but it wasn't a proper visit. I'd like to stroll along the boardwalk and watch the performance artists.

— What about another visit to the dinosaurs? Are there any dinosaurs on Pedraterra?

— Only human ones.

— I'm not a dinosaur anymore. You children and Petra are reinforcing my inner child, animating my old bones.

— The child hardly needs reinforcing, says Petra, smiling.

— We could also go on a tour of Hollywood, and visit the Planetarium and La Brea Tarpits, and the Science Centre if there is time. Tracy from Coffee Bean would show us round the Getty Museum. It would be interesting to see her with her other hat on. And there's baseball.

— We watched it on TV before we went to Pedraterra. It was OK. But I prefer basketball, says Gemma.

— Me too. I play basketball for the junior county in Dunedin. Cricket's your favourite sport, grandpa, isn't it?

— Yes, but it's very amateur over here. I would love to take Petra to a match and explain the rules. As we're in Los Angeles, it might be fun to go to the Dodgers and watch baseball, just for the experience, and eat hot dogs and popcorn. Are you up for that, Petra, Gemma, Peter?

— Count me in, said Gemma.

— Me too, said Peter.

— I am a citizen of nowhere, I need to find out how the other half lives. I'll never go native. I'm fine with that. It's one world and one climate and while I'm in LA, I'll support the Dodgers. Let's do it.

— Then, as I said, there's the planetarium, the science centre, the La Brea tar pits. This is a great city, the first one in the world which presupposed the automobile. There is no shortage of things to do, you just have to get to them.

— What about the pebble room?

Peter's remark startles me, but I don't show it, and I don't catch Petra's eye. The children get up from the table: they're going to play chess and then chill out in front of the TV until bedtime. We go to my study with a bottle of wine. When the children are asleep, it will be time for unfinished business.

I peep into their room. Sound asleep. Funny phrase that. I return to my office and put on Dinu Lipatti's final recital, Lipatti the greatest pianist of them all, Lipatti who knew he was dying: Bach, Mozart, Schubert, Chopin. A dress rehearsal for my own death. Why do we die? A combination of reasons. All deaths — not only suicides — are over-determined. We can make a stab at listing the reasons, including the strictly medical, often cruel and certainly decisive. What we cannot know is the percentage, the value-added surplus. Who knows whether a particular act of cruelty tips a person over the edge, but a little later than might have been expected thanks to a counterbalancing act of kindness? The modalities of heartbreak — and also of privilege, since I am talking about the otherwise healthy. I have a large glass of Saint-Émilion, the wine my father — whose forgiveness I beg for my failure to appreciate his goodness — liked best, and smile at Petra.

9.

— Where were we, my dear Petra?

— *Don Giovanni*, the Stone Guest.

— Earlier, I was wondering what I could not live without: Petra; grandchildren and their families; writing; stone. It's a paradox: without my pebble room I would have had no access to Pedraterra and no Petra, at least not as part of my lived life. There is something lifeless about Pedraterra: the rigidity, the lifelessness, the surveillance, these are embodied in the way stone symbolises and realises and embodies the culture and folkways of the people and will one day destroy the country, unless there is a revolution. Perhaps there are others like you, perhaps even now they are planning an uprising. Is it your destiny to lead the revolution? I don't want to believe that I must abandon all thought of stone. My heart is not stony. You would not make love to a stony-hearted man. I have introjected the beauty and simplicity, the colour and eternity of pebbles. They are central to the ecology of the world, to the ecology of mind. My collection is something special. But it does not have to remain here. I will bequeath it to a great museum.

— Go on.

— Better yet, I'll donate the pebbles as soon as possible. You need a room of your own, because one day you will create a great work. Soon the pebble room will be empty. If you don't want it as your study, I will move my office there, and you'll have yours here, where we first made love.

 Judging the risk of disturbance from the children to be very low, I take off my clothes. Petra does the same. We make love to the music of Chopin. I burst into tears. Petra takes me to her breast and holds me tight. We dress and return to our chairs.

— Dear Dunstan. I deeply appreciate your lucidity and resolution. I might even agree to taking over your office but your hard work on your mentality has had the unexpected and immediate effect of releasing me from my demons. Maybe your pebble room would be the right place for me to work, to plan the revolution by the secret door. Don't look so alarmed, I'm only joking. If I ever went back to Pedraterra, you would be with me and the circumstances would be very different. There is something else to determine: the kind of book you are going to write. Put on *Don Giovanni* again.

— I'll find the commendatore. Listen.

— I'm listening and I'm waiting for your thoughts about the book.

— Waiting. That's what we do with music. It idealises time, just as painting idealises space. We listen to great music, because we are going to die, because we are learning how to die. It's not primarily an emotional experience or an intellectual experience or an aesthetic experience, it's an existential experience, a pilgrimage.

— You put it well. I had never thought about music in those terms. I had never thought about music full stop. Even so, you have years to go before you die. And your first task is to write the book.

— I know but I'm not sure I can manage a novel. Travel books are easier.

— Unless....

— Neither?

— Try again.

— Both.

— You're getting closer.

— Ah, a novel in the form of a travel book or a travel book in the form of a novel? For sure, there are many fictional representations of place.

— Think about a place which — without material evidence in the form of clothes and bowls and rock – you might come to feel you had imagined thanks to your fertile sense of stone, your pebble world of the mind.

— Pedraterra. Write about Pedraterra — a whole book about Pedraterra. Is this what I have to do? But it's not either/or, is it? Either/or involves absolute choices, like finding a partner…. An account of Pedraterra could be the introduction to a book of imaginary countries, couldn't it? It would be followed by sections about countries where the fundamental element is something other than stone: water, fabrics, fire, earth. Then there would be an account of my pebbles. The book could conclude with an essay I have always wanted to write, about the atmospheric role of place in fiction and movies: black and white French films of the 1940s, Sebald, Dostoevsky, *Nostromo*, *Ulysses*. So, a three-part book. It's time to plan the remainder of the children's stay.

— Pride of place is a visit to Craig. I'm a changed woman, thanks to you. I want to see how a lithograph is made. Yes, I know, stone! Would Craig do a drawing of me, and make a print which would join the ones of you and the children? What kind of paintings does he do?

— Long, thin ones, vertical rather than horizontal, portrait rather than landscape. I'm sure he'd be delighted to do a drawing of you.

— What does he use?

— Pastel, acrylics, pen and ink. He's a traditional modernist, a master. Why don't we set it up first thing in the morning?

We are exhausted. I prepare hot toddies: red wine, lemon, honey, cinnamon. Drinking our nightcaps, I put on Lipatti playing the Mozart sonata in A minor.

— By the way, how did you manage to trick the surveillance?

— Easy. They are not as efficient as they think. This is their weakest link.

We kiss and go to our separate bedrooms.

10.

The next few days pass in a whirl. We visit all the places and do all the things which had been proposed. On the way to the Getty, we pass by the Coffee Bean, as arranged, to collect Tracy, who has agreed to accompany us. Petra admits she had been momentarily jealous of her but knows very well I only have eyes for Petra Sandstone, Petra from Pedraterra. It's a funny old world. Or new world. During the short drive to the museum it emerges that Tracy is an enormous admirer of Craig's work. She knows him well from the Coffee Bean.

— I'm a *close* friend of Piotr.

— You mean you love each other, says Gemma.

— He never says anything, says Peter.

— That's right, he's strong and silent.

Tracy's tour is perfectly pitched to interest all the visitors. I suddenly realise I could have a word about my pebble collection with a curator I know. After the tour, we walk across to the cafeteria. I say I need to speak to someone who works here. Petra will explain. I call him on my mobile.

— James, it's Dunstan. I'm at the Museum. Have you got five minutes? I need to discuss something important with you.

— I'll be with you before you put down the phone. For you, I have half an hour. That's easier to arrange than five minutes.

— Ha ha, I recognise the allusion to Henry James or is it Thoreau. Let's go for a stroll, away from the cafeteria where my family will be watching us.

— What's so important?

— I know you admire my pebble collection. I want to donate it immediately to a great museum. I am inclined to favour the Getty, mainly because Los Angeles is where I live. Find me a brilliant curator who will prepare a catalogue raisonné of the pebbles with my help.

— I am well aware of the love and knowledge behind the collection. It's a noble gesture to offer the collection to us and, given the Museum's big involvement in archaeology and the ancient world, there could well be a positive response. In particular, it could suit our Research Institute. Email me with a proposal and I'll forward it to the appropriate person who in turn will have to persuade the relevant committee.

We take our leave. I know it's the right decision. Out of my hands, in the the lap of the gods, the members of the committee. Before entering the cafeteria, I take out my mobile.

— Hi Craig, we'd like to visit the studio again.

— Tomorrow?

— Yes, that's perfect. I'm bringing "my new friend", Petra.

Craig is a practised man of the world and knows what my phrase signifies, especially in my case, as I have been partnerless for several years. This has never happened to Craig, who is a member of the opposite tendency.

The next day we drive to Craig's studio and, as Gemma requested, we stop first at the Venice boardwalk so that she and Petra can see the performance artists Peter saw immediately after his arrival.

Piotr greets us on arrival at the studio because Craig is on the phone. I look at the silent printer in a different way now that I know he is Tracy's boyfriend. Craig comes off the phone and eyes Petra approvingly. A new lover is always interested in the partner's best friend, and Petra in turn studies Craig with interest. He embraces us and high-fives Peter and Gemma.

Before Craig can start asking questions, the cousins repeat their half-serious request from the other day: to be drawn while standing on one leg and, as Peter said, "climbing a pebble". I chip in with a request that Craig draw and make a print of Petra, to accompany the one he did of the children, and the one he did of me a few years ago. No one else in the world would ask Craig to make works on the spur of the moment but no one else in the world is Craig's best friend.

— Can you hold the pose for ten or fifteen minutes without support? It's OK, I'm only teasing.

You can have support and I'll draw it so that it looks as though you are without any. With his customary grace and speed Craig draws Peter and Gemma together, each standing on one leg, with Peter's foot uncomfortably on a pebble. Peter's own idea, so he can't complain! Now it's time to draw Petra. Once again, Craig's extraordinary skill as a draughtsman, equal some say to Raphael, is on display: the holy trinity of brain and eye and hand. After everyone has expressed admiration, he hands the two drawings to Piotr and they set to work on the prepared stone. An hour later, six copies have been made of both drawings.

Gemma's London flight is leaving at 21.35pm, Peter's Auckland flight at 22.30pm. Just enough time to say goodbye to each of them individually and without fuss. We did the emotional stuff at my house. Peter and Gemma are beginning to focus on home. Peter's flight will take about thirteen hours, Gemma's eleven: two long hauls. They have digital equipment and books. Their prints are rolled up and safe in tubes.

ANGLETERRE

"The secret things belong unto the Lord our God; but the things that are revealed belong unto us and to our children for ever" (*Deuteronomy* **XXIX**, verse 28).

1.

A dormitory at the Jansenist college of Port-Royal-des-Champs near Paris on a bitterly cold morning early in 1656 was no place for a new student to wake up. Even an exemplary student is human, with his doubts, his torments, his gooseflesh, and it is certain that the first thoughts of the young man in question, Jean Racine, did not touch upon the doctrines of predestination, original sin and divine grace, which were often debated at Port-Royal. Given that this was the worst winter for many years, it followed ineluctably that the washrooms were even colder than usual. At this unholy hour, he did not warm to the new day. Racine's parents had both died before he was three years old. The orphan's maternal grandmother had accepted responsibility for his well-being and education, and she entrusted him to the Jansenists of Port-Royal, in conformity with her strict religious beliefs.

It was not written in the college curriculum that the young man would become a playwright of genius. He might easily have ended up a wrangler with inferior things: court intrigues, casuistry and the like. Creative achievement of the order (*le mot juste*) of Jean Racine — *"Le classique par excellence"*, as Jules Lemaître would say to his friend Stéphane Mallarmé at the poet's regular salon, 89 rue de Rome, Paris 8e, one Tuesday evening in 1888 — involves seizing and elaborating, at a given *and* appropriate psycho-historical moment, the most complex and difficult of the finite matrixial possibilities theoretically available to all willing to take the plunge. But writing was in Racine's blood, and that was what he had to do. Let others worry their heads about posterity. In any case, "foreknowledge is as helpful as cupping a corpse": such was the opinion of Jean's tutor at the college, Antoine (Angelo) Oltrarno, a Florence-born Marrano and former denizen of Amsterdam. More often than not, Oltrarno would saddle this opinion with a rider: "in any event, the future is unfated". Nonetheless, Racine's education in the classics, especially Greek language and literature, was central to his development.

2.

Back in 1639, the year of Racine's birth, Antoine
Oltrarno, aged twenty, arrived in Paris from
Amsterdam, where he had lodged with his second
cousin, Rabbi Menasseh ben Israel. In Amsterdam,
the self-confident and high-powered Oltrarno had
been caught up in the intellectual and religious
ferment coursing through the town's Jewish
community, symbolised on the one hand by the
famous or infamous free-thinker Uriel Acosta and,
on the other hand, by renewed Jewish interest in
mystical cults, especially the Kabbalah. No one in
Amsterdam could have predicted Baruch Spinoza's
philosophy or Shabbetai Tzvi's Messianic onslaught,
both of which would henceforth have a huge impact
on publicly declared Jews and their Marrano
brethren everywhere, including Oltrarno, whose
spiritual life had been seriously destabilised by these
developments – to the point that he sought out the
Jesuits in Paris. Teaching him the knowledge, they
almost persuaded him to join them, but something
was lacking so he waited. Then, crucially, he met the
ex-Huguenot theologian Sacy and found himself
drawn, as if by a magnet, towards the thought and

practice of Cornelius Jansenius. Sacy, however, realised while discussing his ongoing translation of the Old Testament with his new friend, that, unconsciously, Oltrarno remained the Jew he had always been: "Marrano" therefore was an accurate description of his soul, as Antoine's student Jean Racine would later intuit.

Oltrarno could be brutally pragmatic: "what you do is get up in the morning, even the coldest morning, and nail your buttocks to the chair. *Laborare est orare*, as the Benedictines say." His fellow-Jansenists at Port-Royal, the most intellectually rigorous Catholics since Aquinas or even the heretical Donatists, suspected Antoine of being heterodox, and whispers of "a contradiction in terms" were occasionally heard. In the small hours, Oltrarno would tell himself that he definitely *was* a Jansenist — only to banish the implications of this night thought as quickly as possible from his troubled mind: the Duc de la Rochefoucauld would certainly compose a maxim inspired by his friend's complex aporias if these were ever to become public knowledge.

The day was certainly not purer than the depths of Racine's heart, which did not prevent him from groaning — like a stocking-knitter with a heavy period — at the coldness of the winter morning. And then, oh yes, he did get out of bed. On some level, as yet unexplored, Jean Racine knew that freedom was the recognition of necessity. Even in the depths of winter he sensed that Port-Royal, irrespective of theological considerations, was the best place for a vulnerable orphan to nourish his artistic vocation.

3.

In 1653, before embarking on a long-desired journey to London in search of information about one of his abiding interests, namely the suppressed Order of the Knights Templar – the Cistercian nuns at Port-Royal greatly admired Bernard of Clairvaux — Antoine Oltrarno decided, on sentimental grounds, to revisit Amsterdam. There, as in 1639, he stayed with Menasseh ben Israel himself, who spun an unlikely yarn about his plans, which were well advanced, to persuade the new ruler of England, Oliver Cromwell, to allow the Jews to return whence they had been expelled by King Edward the First in 1290. Menasseh, who regretted no longer having the time to teach at Amsterdam's famous Marrano School, talked at length about his best students and introduced Oltrarno to the brightest star in his scholarly firmament, Baruch Spinoza, who for the time being was working in the family business, while associating with free thinkers.

The following day Menasseh took Oltrarno and Spinoza to meet Rembrandt van Rijn. According to Menasseh's surviving diaries, the great painter made a sketch of the three Jews — now unfortunately lost. That evening, after a long, heated and thoroughly enjoyable discussion on Jewish destiny — specifically about tension between collective and individual representations of the intellect and of the soul in the writings of Maimonides and other great Jewish and Islamic thinkers — Oltrarno suggested to the precocious Spinoza that he visit France: even Baruch Spinoza, already in trouble with the Jewish community, could use a change of scenery and Antoine would introduce him to Pascal, who visited Port-Royal from time to time.

The next morning Antoine was introduced by Spinoza to Richard Oliver, a former member of the English Puritan sect known as the Men of the Fifth Monarchy. Richard Oliver, whose religious obsessions had led him to the worlds of Jewish prophecy and Kabbalah, explained to Antoine that he was converting to Judaism under the auspices of Rabbi Saul Morteira, an Italian Jew, former teacher of Spinoza and member of the Amsterdam *Beth Din* or rabbinical court, which was later to excommunicate the great philosopher. Oliver had left the ranks of the Fifth Monarchists because the results of his studies were incompatible with the sect's theology which, like that of Comenius, required the conversion of the Jews to Christianity.

On learning that Antoine was going to London to research the Knights Templar, Richard told the visitor that his brother, Sydney, owned a bookshop in The Temple. The Temple was the site of the old Templars building, and Sydney might well have a book on the subject. Antoine was to greet him and explain that the rabbinical court had directed that he, Richard, would only need to have a symbolic circumcision as he had been born, like Adam and certain angels, without a foreskin. Richard himself was conducting studies into angels. He told Oltrarno that the fourteenth century Kabbalists who had calculated that there were 301,655,722 angels had got it wrong, but he was not yet ready to say by how many.

4.

After returning to Paris where he attended to his devotions and checked his notes on the Knights Templar, Antoine made his way to London, which his Port-Royal colleague, Terence François, had described to him as an "unreal city… The river sweats oil and tar". Terence had explained where to make for after the coach arrived at the river. Antoine crossed London Bridge and walked to Creechurch Lane in the City, coincidentally near the small and illegal synagogue where Marranos worshipped, and which Samuel Pepys would famously visit ten years later. In Creechurch Lane, Antoine was welcomed at the lodgings Terence had recommended.

After an excellent night's sleep, Oltrarno rose early and walked along Cheapside before zigzagging his way through small side streets till he reached the Thames Embankment. Finally arriving at the Temple, he found the bookshop owned by Sydney Oliver, and passed on Richard's message about circumcision. Sydney, gently tugging his left eyelid, gave the visitor a look as if to say: "I'm not in the least surprised, Richard was mad to start with", and then directed Antoine to a shelf in the back room on which he would find books and pamphlets about the Knights Templar. After introducing him to a lawyer friend who was browsing at the front of the shop, Sydney Oliver gave him the name of a scholar in Oxford to whom he could write about the proscribed Order. Antoine chose a few items about the Knights Templar and then moved on to another shelf, where he found a copy of Plutarch's *Lives* in North's translation and also in Amyot's French translation on which North's was based. Partly hidden behind them were two copies of the Second Folio of Shakespeare, a work too dangerous to display prominently during what would later become known as the Interregnum. Word having already reached Paris about Shakespeare – although it would be a hundred and sixteen years before a play by him, namely *Hamlet*, was performed in Paris — the learned visitor purchased one of the two Folios and the two Plutarch volumes. Then having rested, walked around some more, stopped off in one of those brand new coffee houses and prayed to his God by the river, he returned to Creechurch Lane.

There, whom should he bump into but a certain Esteban Cangas de Onis y del Mercea, who turned out to be a second cousin once removed of Oltrarno's father? Esteban told Antoine that London Marranos were agog with excitement about his own and Antoine's mutual relative Menasseh Ben Israel's forthcoming initiatives. Oltrarno spent a couple of days enjoying the hospitality of this small group of semi-secret Jews and attempted to explain Jansenism to them. Not entirely to his surprise, he was told by Felusz Raphael, the Polish brother-in-law of Esteban and said to be the only Ashkenazi Jew in London, that since Jansenism was a branch of Christianity, it was not for the Jews, thank you very much. Felusz had fled Poland during the Chmelnitzky massacres of Jews of 1648 and 1649 in neighbouring Ukraine, a wise precaution given that many thousands had been slaughtered during the reign of terror. Oltrarno was tempted to suggest that subscribing to the "wrong" religion was preferable to being murdered by a marauding Cossack but resisted the suggestion since Felusz would argue that this was an academic point, even casuistical, which of course it was.

At the end of his stay Antoine was escorted to the Canterbury/Dover coach by Esteban and two new Marrano friends of Esteban, twin brothers who had only recently arrived in London. These gentlemen were from the Canary Islands, merchants by day and Kabbalists by night.

5.

One lonely evening, soon after his return to France, Antoine Angelo was beset by a great yearning to visit his parents, Joseph and Miriam, and his twin brother David, in Florence. This yearning overwhelmed him and he burst into tears. He saw his family coloured and he saw his family plain and he remembered his childhood with great nostalgia. Originating in the Portuguese Marrano community, his parents did not live within the ghetto — five minutes' walk from the Duomo — but just outside it, above the shop where they scraped a living as second-hand clothes dealers. When someone died in or near the ghetto, they would buy the late-lamented's clothes, known as *shmutters*, and sell them on.

Antoine longed to hear his father singing Arab Andalousian *hawzi* songs (taught to him by a Spanish Marrano who looked like one of the merchant friends of Esteban), while accompanying himself on the mandolin. He remembered how his mother would throw a piece of dough back in the fire after baking bread, and his mouth watered for her *caponata all'ebraica*, an eggplant dish cooked in capers which her great-great-great-grandmother had been taught by a Sicilian relative who, after the Jews were expelled from Sicily in 1492, came via Naples to Florence, where the Inquisition was mild. There was, indeed, a family rumour that Michelangelo himself had tasted the dish — as cooked by the said ancestor — at a party to celebrate the culmination of the great sculptor's magnificent *David*.

In this mood, while brooding on the broken segue of family life, Antoine Oltrarno always derived comfort from his family tree. To his amazement, he noticed for the first time that the names of a remote ancestor from the Azores, Guillermo Shakespires, were a Portuguese version of William Shakespeare. Thanks to this spectacular coincidence, his *saudade* (the Portuguese word for melancholy yearning often used by his parents) vanished into the future. Cheerful again, Oltrarno decided he would return to England as soon as possible.

Sometime late in 1654, Antoine learned from his young friend Baruch Spinoza — who had come to Port-Royal for a week in order to escape the stresses and strains of his troubled existence in Amsterdam and, thanks to Antoine, had finally been introduced to Blaise Pascal — that Antoine's relative, Rabbi Menasseh Ben Israel, was making genuine headway with his extraordinary campaign to persuade Oliver Cromwell that the Jews should be permitted by law to return to England. Antoine was fascinated by these developments and putting his interest in the Knights Templar on the back burner, resolved to explore the matter further. Like Pascal he was obsessed by Jewish fate. Unlike Pascal he *was*, deep down, a Jew.

One evening, Antoine excused himself, he had work to do. Alone together for the first time, Spinoza and Pascal made small talk for about two minutes, and then fell silent. However, Pascal had a brainwave, a classic solution to awkwardness: the royal game, chess, 1) P-K4/P-K4, 2) K-KB3/K-QB3, 3) B-K5 were the opening moves. By the time Antoine rejoined them, they were already in friendly discussion. A fascinated Pascal (who had already penned but not yet published his *Pensées*) was listening carefully while Spinoza spoke in some detail about what was going on in Amsterdam. The younger man's situation there was very difficult not only because of his rationalist views ("a thinking reed" par excellence) but also because the insecure Jewish community felt threatened by his attitude to his late father's gentile creditors, whom he was outwitting in the run-up to a court case. He explained that it was likely he would soon be excluded from the local community, but that he would never grovel to the synagogue, nor would he convert to Christianity. He would stay on in Amsterdam, not Jewish by religion, not Christian, not Marrano: a man. This was a man; the very model of a modern man; the first modern Jew. Had they known this, the irony would not have been lost on any of them.

6.

In March 1656, without telling anyone at Port-Royal his real reason for the journey, Antoine made arrangements for a second and doubtless final visit to London. First, however, he would go to Florence, for the long-awaited homecoming, after seventeen years away. No mention was made of Jansenism and everybody made a fuss of him, then his dear mother fed him her superb *caponata* and his father sang his beloved *hawzi* songs. Angelo, as they all called Antoine, prayed fervently in the Brancacci Chapel; he then spent a long time before the great frescoes, in particular Masaccio's *Adam and Eve*. But was Port-Royal really Eden? he wondered, as he left for London.

After a short stay in London, where the status of Jews was at last as good as legal, he returned home to Paris not only with the other copy of Shakespeare's plays — still unsold in the Temple bookshop — but also, *ben trovato*, a rare copy of the 1631 Wicked Bible, rumour of which had already reached Paris. Some years later he would smuggle this into the Bastille as a present for his friend, Sacy. Sacy, incarcerated for theological incorrectness, was still working on his translation of the scriptures in the very cell later inhabited by another writer, the Marquis de Sade who, Bastille lore had it, was delighted by the coincidence. Antoine, a fine linguist, knew English (his tenth language after Italian, Ladino, Spanish, Dutch, Hebrew, Arabic, French, Latin and Greek) but he had not been able to attend a performance of Shakespeare in London – no plays had been permitted there since 1642.

7.

Back in Port-Royal, with his curiosity about Shakespeare and Shakespeare's work now modulating into genuine interest, Oltrarno quietly and carefully spent much of his spare time over the next two years studying the plays and explained to his favourite student — who had already surpassed him in Latin and Greek but as yet knew no English — that Shakespeare, certainly England's greatest writer since Chaucer as well as being, it was rumoured, a member of the committee which translated the Holy Bible, did wonderful things in his plays, things which required the English language to embody them ("French, our blessed tongue, is so *essentialist*"). Shakespeare's characters were incandescent with vitality, but the playwright ultimately spoiled the effects by not obeying the proprieties: "On the other hand, he could obey the rules when he wanted to. Read his sonnets — they have the 1640 edition in the Sorbonne library", explained Antoine. "Of course, he knew all about the proprieties: look at the way he presents the first kiss of Romeo and Juliet".

Racine set about learning English so that he could read Shakespeare's plays for himself. Master and student discussed all the aspects of these works — including neglect of propriety — while taking regular and symmetrical walks in the garden at the College. One afternoon, having greeted Racine's aunt at the gate (she was one of the Cistercian nuns at Port-Royal, where she was a close friend of Pascal's sister, also a nun), they left the grounds of the Abbey for their favourite wooded slope, in a beautiful part of the valley about two miles from Port-Royal des Champs. The precocious Racine explained to Antoine that he had been writing poetry — in French and in Latin — for about a year but that his way of seeing the world could no longer be contained in poetry and cried out for the broader canvas of a play. If he did eventually write a play, he for one would naturally obey the proprieties. "A secret is like a woman: it always wears several layers of clothes", he told Antoine, thus anticipating one of his own great themes.

"Remember the time I explained to you that the English language, by virtue of its very nature, encourages Shakespeare's playful attitude towards the proprieties", said Antoine. "For example, his rhythmic inventiveness, his lexical prodigality, have their roots in the interaction of Anglo-Saxon and Latinate words."

"True," said Racine. "But the unities propose a centripetal *imaginaire*, as in painting. Break them, and you end up with the opposite, as in music. It is also the case that, unlike painting, words necessarily separate the writer from the original oneness with the mother — and any attempt to use them in order to achieve the opposite aim is vain, hence once more the necessary discipline of the unities. No freedom without straitjackets!"

Returning to the Abbey, they entered the gardens. "Look, Antoine," he continued, "Jenkins is over there, behind the berry tree. A centrifugal *imaginaire* is certainly beyond *his* ken, but it would be interesting to find out if he has heard of William Shakespeare, who is said to be almost as famous in England as Corneille is here." Jenkins was a Welshman, one of two foreign gardeners working at Port-Royal, the other being Johan Sebastian, a short German from Leipzig. Racine had never engaged in conversation with either of them.

"Let's ask him", cried the young man. "Go on", said Antoine, with a twinkle in his eye.

"This is what you must say: `Monsieur Jenkins, 'ave you 'eard of Shakspeer?'". Racine memorised the phrase, practised it on Oltrarno, approached the old man, and politely asked the question. The Welshman's reply was equally polite. "What did Jenkins say?", Jean asked his tutor. Roaring with laughter Antoine said he did not have the faintest idea for, apart from standard greetings in French and English, Jenkins spoke nothing but Welsh. Oltrarno went on: "The only word I caught was *bach*. I wonder if it means 'friend'. He often says '*Bonjour bach*' to the German gardener".

"But I have seen you and other tutors engaged in conversation with Jenkins", said Jean. "How observant you are, possibly too observant", replied Oltrarno, "I wonder what else has caught your eye. You always give proper attention to your studies — but perhaps you have been neglecting your devotions?" They continued their walk. "Let me tell you about Jenkins. Some of my colleagues behave like King Midas, bending the ear of the grain of corn. As if confessing, they pour out their worries to Jenkins, personal and political. Perhaps mild heresies get an airing. He says nothing or replies, politely but briefly, in the language of his fathers. It is not impossible that the learned doctors are pleading for the dark unspoken secrets of their hearts to be forgiven. The sins of men, our *peccata abscondita*, are rarely noised abroad. Perhaps Jenkins senses that his ear is a safety valve".

"I once heard my friend Blaise Pascal attempting, for the first time, to engage in a conversation with him", Oltrarno went on. "I was *not* listening at the keyhole, as it were. No, thinking that Jenkins must be deaf, Pascal was shouting and the whole college could hear". "What in the name of heaven did Doctor Pascal say?", asked Jean, mightily impressed. "Oh, something about love betrayed by ambition, followed by a suggestion that Job chapter 19 verse 25 announces the Christian Messiah. But, as I said, Jenkins is a man of few words. He's as good as his words. I've always thought that the last few verses of Job 19 would make a good aria".

8.

Jean Racine, by far the best student in the College, had time to devote himself to concerns that were not on the syllabus. Shakespeare became an obsession. He asked his fellow *obsédé* to tell him something, anything, about the playwright. Oltrarno thought for a moment and said, "During my second visit to London, after buying the second copy of the Folio, I went for a stroll in the Middle Temple. At the Embankment exit, I recognised the lawyer I had been introduced to on my first visit to the bookshop. He informed me that a great uncle on his mother's side, who had taught William in Stratford-on-Avon, told anybody who would listen that the future writer was brilliant at every subject except Greek, which he could not get the hang of at all, and that he was the most inquisitive and observant student ever to step foot inside his classroom. Maybe coming from a recusant Catholic family on his father's side meant that Shakespeare had learned to keep his eyes open all the time? English intelligencers were crawling about everywhere".

"A pity about Shakespeare's Greek", said Jean pompously. "It's a more likely explanation of his rejection of Aristotle's unities than the nature of the English language. Are *you* a Marrano?", asked Jean slyly? Jean Racine never stopped asking brilliant intuitive questions and now, in a brilliant intuition of his own, Antoine knew that his own student would one day not only become a dramatist, he would become a great one, perhaps France's greatest. "A happy few will make comparisons between Racine and Shakespeare", he said to himself. "Fool, Oltrarno, how can you say such a thing? No, you *can*, you *can*! What look like the seeds of foreknowledge are in fact the fruits of experience. The future *is* unfated." Oltrarno changed the subject. He was not yet ready to discuss his deepest feelings with the precocious Jean, indeed he had not yet come to terms with them himself, reinforced as they had been during and since his second trip *outre-manche*.

By the time Jean Racine left Port-Royal he had taught himself English, and read all Shakespeare's plays in the copy he had borrowed from Oltrarno. The day of his graduation in 1658, Antoine gave it to him as a token of his affection, along with the two volumes of Plutarch, whom Racine knew had been a source for Shakespeare. That night Jean was going with his friend Nicolas Boileau to Molière's new production of *Nicomède* at the Louvre. Antoine, most of whose colleagues did not approve of his passion for theatre, was tempted to accompany the two men to the play; after all it was he who had introduced Jean to the work of Corneille; but he finally decided to stay at home. Before supper he sat in the garden with his remaining copy of Shakespeare. After reading *The Merchant of Venice* for half an hour, he approached Jenkins, to bend his Welsh ear.

The rest is silence, but Benedict Spinoza, finally excluded from the Amsterdam Jewish community and who had recently turned down an offer from the Sun King to be court philosopher at the Palace of Versailles — was on Antoine's mind, as was Richard Oliver: Sydney Oliver, with whom Antoine was in correspondence about *The Merchant of Venice*, had recently written from his bookshop in the Temple that his brother was now a fully-fledged Jew.

9.

Jean Racine broke with Port-Royal more or less definitively in the early sixteen sixties. Between 1667 and 1677 he wrote seven of his eight masterpieces. After the failure of *Phèdre* and *Hyppolyte* in 1677, he renounced what his hard-line colleagues saw as the frivolity of theatre. He spent the next twelve years raising a family with a holy (and wealthy) woman who thoroughly disapproved of theatre and had never read or seen a single one of his plays. Four of his five daughters became nuns. As a reward for service to the arts, and despite the King's suspicions of Jansenist heresy, Racine was appointed the King's historiographer.

10.

In 1689, Racine returned to the theatre. Madame de Maintenon, granddaughter of the great Huguenot poet Agrippa d'Aubigné and morganatic second wife of Louis XIV (a great improvement on her legless and lecherous first husband, the writer Paul Scarron), commissioned Racine to write a verse drama for her students. Her educational activities were under the protection of the King. The drama was to be performed as a school play by the genteel but impoverished girls for whom Madame's school in Saint-Cyr was set up. The language of the school's charter — drawn up by Mme de Maintenon and the king – had been checked by Racine who also wrote the words inscribed on the crosses worn by the girls. For the subject of his play Racine, after consulting his friend Boileau, chose Queen Esther, the first time in his career he had quarried the Bible for a story — something Shakespeare, who often alluded to Biblical phrases and was well read in the (Geneva) bible – never did. Bossuet and La Rochefoucauld were present at the first performance, the exiled King James II of England at the third, Madame de Sévigné — who loved the play — at the fifth. Some people thought they detected a parallel between Esther and Vashti on the one hand and Mesdames de Maintenon and de Montespan (her predecessor at court) on the other, not to mention the stage King and the real King. Some people were right. The play was a great success, with the beautiful voice of Madeleine de Glapion (later to be headmistress of Saint-Cyr) in the trouser role of Mordechai. Racine, praised by one and all, prayed in chapel for his pride to be removed, his glory to set up residence elsewhere.

Thinking about the preface to the first printed version of this, his penultimate play, Jean wrote to his former teacher, asking if they could meet soon. A few months earlier Racine had learned from a mutual friend, his relative by marriage, Jean de la Fontaine, that in 1686 Antoine Oltrarno had returned to the faith of his ancestors, despite the dangers attendant upon remaining in a country which expelled the Huguenots after Louis XIV's revocation of the Edict of Nantes in the previous year, having already expelled most of the Jews some years prior to that. Minorities were barely tolerated in France. Only in Lorraine was it reasonably safe to practise the Jewish religion. A quiet word from Racine to Madame de

Maintenon, however, ensured the protection and safety of Antoine, possibly the only person in Paris living more or less openly as a Jew.

11.

During his teens Oltrarno had been unhappy with life in Florence, where not only was there conflict between traditional Jews and those of Marrano descent, but free intellectual enquiry was seen as heralding a full-on Jewish reformation, which was to be avoided at all costs. True there were no ghetto Jews in Livorno, where Marranos were protected and Portuguese was the official language of the community. Nor were there any in Pisa, and these were the only cities of Jewish settlement in Europe without ghettos. But, like other young radicals, Oltrarno was keen to sharpen his wits on the cutting edge of Jewish mind and Jewish existence and, as indicated earlier, left for Amsterdam in 1639, the year of Racine's birth. No other city could compete with Amsterdam. Dutch Brazil, open to immigration, certainly had its attractions, in particular a beautiful marriageable cousin, but cutting edge it wasn't. Every Jewish possibility was available in Amsterdam, provided you publicly kept to the rules.

However, in 1640, it can now be revealed, Oltrarno had a traumatic experience in Amsterdam which he did his best to put out of sight of his mind's eye: he witnessed the public penitential whipping, at the threshold of the synagogue, of Uriel Acosta, the former Marrano, born in Oporto and later a minor church official in the university city of Coimbra. There, before leaving for Amsterdam, Acosta befriended Professor Homem, the homosexual Marrano theologian and secret rabbi, later betrayed by a colleague to the Inquisition and burned at the stake after being told by his interrogator that he was not even a good Jew, because Jews didn't do what he said they did. The intolerance shown towards Acosta — a learned, brilliant, subtle, energetic, tormented rationalist freethinker — by the Jewish community, led Oltrarno to an agonising reappraisal concerning his ancestral Judaism. Despite being only eight years old at the time, Spinoza had been taken to see the whipping. Oltrarno remembered the look in Spinoza's eye when, in Paris, the philosopher recounted this episode.

Oltrarno's spiritual needs could be met neither by freethinking abandonment of religion nor by the world of the Jewish fundamentalist persecutors of freethinking. He had no option but to remain a Marrano — after all, Marrano tradition has it that the Messiah will be one of their number, unrecognisable to openly declared Jews – or even become a devout and pious Catholic. Had Antoine stayed on in Amsterdam he would have been faced with the option of taking the eventual direction of Spinoza or of coming to terms with the Jewish establishment and, who knows, joining the group of six hundred faithful led by a senior follower of Shabbetai Zvi, Rabbi Aboab de Fonseca (he was also the former teacher of Baruch Spinoza and his future excommunicator), who emigrated to Brazil in 1641. Had Oltrano gone to Brazil, he would certainly have set up a Jewish home with his marriageable cousin, Beatrice Bianca Sheps. He might have sought out the descendants of the ten lost tribes in Quito, Ecuador, who were to become yet another of his great interests later on. But thirteen years older than his future friend Baruch Spinoza and possessing a very different mindset, Oltrarno left for France. If Amsterdam housed the Jewish ferment of Europe, Paris would open doors to a new Christian world.

12.

Antoine came home. Perhaps he had never left. Inner and outer worlds were at now at one with each other. The *mitzvot*, the commandments, moved from the small back room to the front parlour. They had become his raison d'être. Jean Racine and Antoine Angel Oltrarno had the first of several documented post-Port-Royal meetings on a Friday in the autumn of 1689, their seventieth and fiftieth year respectively. It took place in Oltrarno's Left Bank house, 6 rue des Grands-Augustins. The two men embraced. "Thirty years, Antoine, thirty years". The old man smiled: "I am also known as Malachi, which is my synagogue name – not that there is a synagogue to attend. It is the Hebrew for mio Angelo. Malachi ben-Joseph. Let us have some tea and calvados".

After their refreshments, they went to Antoine Malachi's study, where Racine squinted at the *mezuza* on the door and at the older man's phylacteries on his desk, wondering what they were. "I have followed your career over the years", said Antoine, "and I well remember our conversations in the garden at Port-Royal. Perhaps your readings of Shakespeare influenced your style in the opposite direction. You certainly respect the unities! I remember too your early poems: "Our nights: they are more lovely than your days...."

"I am most grateful to you, dear Antoine. Shakespeare is a shining light, but his work reinforced my belief, as I told you at the time, that if ever I wrote plays I would respect the unities. This maximises the power of the content. I also went to the library of the Sorbonne, as you suggested, to read the sonnets. They are much more powerful than even the best by Du Bellay, Ronsard and Camões. Perhaps one day a great poet will translate them. I myself had a go at translating number 73 but I couldn't fit it into fourteen lines."

Esther was, in effect, a musical, for the King encouraged Molière and Racine to integrate music into their plays. The music was by Jean's friend, Jean-Baptiste Moreau, whose setting, particularly of the final chorus, had been criticised by certain courtiers until Madame shut them up. Racine, ultra-sensitive to even the mildest criticism after his long absence from theatre, felt he had to defend every single aspect of the Saint-Cyr production in his forthcoming preface to the published version of the play. Perhaps the deep reason why he felt such a strong impulse to explain and protect the production was that he had never forgotten how critical — with the best of intentions — his family and teachers, including Antoine, could be.

Jean explained his problem concerning the preface to Antoine, who suggested that he should associate his play with the famous Biblical songs of praise of Miriam, Deborah and Judith, three *loci classici* of Jewish thanksgiving. Racine followed his advice in the penultimate sentence of the preface. The preface concludes with a verbatim quote from Antoine although he would not permit a direct acknowledgment: "It is said that even in our time the Jews celebrate with great expressions of thanksgiving the day when their ancestors were delivered by Esther from the cruelty of Haman". Antoine described Esther as the first Marrano — and indeed she was a symbol of resistance in the hearts of Marranos for centuries — but he would not let Racine include the phrase in his preface.

One day, long in the future, Louis-Ferdinand Céline would say that *Esther* and *Athalie* were nothing but "a vehement apologia for *la Juiverie*". Voltaire, on the other hand, thought *Athalie* was the greatest triumph of the human spirit, the supreme masterpiece of all time. Be that as it may, *Athalie*, Racine's eighth great play and his final work for the theatre, may well have been inspired by Malachi's publicly expressed return to his Jewish roots. Does not Athalie say in scene six of the final act that God opposed her to herself twenty times in one day? There can be no doubt that Antoine Malachi and Jean discussed the relationship between Judaism and Christianity. In a letter to Madame de Maintenon, Jean de La Fontaine wrote that the two men found plenty of food for thought in Pascal's celebrated comments on the Jewish religion: dear Pascal, to whom the young Racine had been introduced by Malachi shortly before Jean left Port-Royal in 1659. One such comment, indeed, is quoted in La Fontaine's letter: "Anyone who judges the religion of the Jews by its cruder adherents has little knowledge of it". The play, in Racine's lifetime, was only performed in Madame's private apartment. Things had worsened in the two years since the triumph of *Esther*.

13.

Jean and Malachi met on a Friday afternoon. "Soon it will be time for me to greet the bride of Israel, the holy Sabbath which, the ancient rabbis tell us, is a foretaste of the world to come", said Malachi. "Let me tell you the rest of the story about my second trip to London, which was in 1656. For my own reasons, I kept this part of it to myself all these years. After my first trip to London, I was studying my family tree. I noticed that in the late fifteenth century there was a certain Guillermo Shakespires, head of the Marrano community in Ribeira Grande on the island of San Miguel in the Azores. Later, I did some research and discovered he was a prodigious writer of sonnets (his wife, Maria-João, was a harpsichord-ist). I had been feeling rather sorry for myself, but the extraordinary coincidence of names cheered me up. I decided there and then to return to London."

"This second trip led me to my foundational self, to the Jewish Angelo Antoine, to the burning bush of my own soul. The undeniable fact is that I am what Shakespeare's Falstaff calls 'an 'ebrew Jew'. You see, apart from small groups of Marranos, there were hardly any Jews in England, and none officially, for around three and a half centuries, since the expulsion in 1290. But northern Europe has decided it can live with Jews and — in the last forty or fifty years — they have started to return to England in small numbers. They are to be found mainly in Bristol, and in the central area and east end of the City of London. I was lucky enough to get to know one of them. His family had been in England since the time of Queen Elizabeth. Remember I told you about a lawyer I first met three years earlier in the bookshop in Middle Temple, the one whose great-uncle had taught William Shakespeare? Well, as we strolled along the Thames Embankment, the good fellow imparted some information to me which would eventually change my life".

"Only a few months earlier Cromwell had received the *Humble Addresses* of Rabbi Menasseh ben Israel of Amsterdam, concerning the readmission of the Jews to England. This encounter led to the historic Whitehall Conference in December. Rabbi Menasseh's reasoning was theological: Jews *must* live in England again because the Messiah cannot redeem humanity until the chosen people are found again everywhere. His proof texts are *Daniel* XII verse 7, *Deuteronomy* XXX verse 4 and, above all, *Deuteronomy* XXVIII, verse 64: `And the Lord shall scatter you among all peoples, from the one end of the earth even unto the other end of the earth'. *K'tse ha'aretz*, end of the earth, England, *Angleterre. Quod erat demonstrandum.* He mentioned that the Hindu ruler of Cochin and his Jews were very happy with each other. I tell you, Jean, Menasseh's messianic dreams rival those of Athalie's husband! And I tell you something else, messianic speculation was rife in London, according to Sydney Oliver the bookseller, among groups like the Men of the Fifth Monarchy to which his brother Richard belonged, until he converted to Judaism."

"Then the lawyer released a thunderbolt, namely that 'this very day Menasseh Ben Israel, who is a second cousin of mine, is to sign a petition of the London Marranos to Cromwell. Rabbi Menasseh is a *rara avis*, a fanatical mystic and a practical politician all at once. There is no doubt about it', said the lawyer with a quiet glow of excitement, 'there is no doubt about it, our people are returning to England. Within a generation Jews will be living here openly. Surely God is to be praised.'"

"'How incredible that I should bump into and recognise a fellow Marrano in the Middle Temple!', I said to him, 'but first, what is your name?' 'Lopes, Nathaniel Roderigo (known as Ruy) Lopes, Roderigo named for my paternal great-grandfather, who was brought to England by Sir Francis Drake and later executed by Queen Elizabeth. Ruy Lopes was the Queen's physician, but the Earl of Essex took a dislike to him and told the Queen he did not trust the doctor, whom he described as a quack. Ruy was a mere pawn in someone else's endgame. His brother-in-law was Hector Nunes, who had given Sir Francis Walsingham the first news of the Great Armada's arrival at Lisbon. As for me, I don't believe the theory that Shylock is based on Ruy. Nor do I believe that Emilia Bassano is a Jewess *or* the dark lady of Shakespeare's sonnets for that matter'".

"'This is beyond belief. Listen, Ruy, if I were a pagan I would read significance into what is mere coincidence, and convenient coincidence at that: I myself am a second cousin of Menasseh ben Israel and, who knows, maybe you and I are related too! Let's explore the genealogical details later, but now, where can we find Menasseh in this great city?'"

"Ruy Lopes quickened his step. 'I am to have dinner with him, and a London cousin, Esteban Cangas de Onis, this very evening. Benjamin Disraeli Pinto-Lopes late of Amsterdam, a confidant and relative of Menasseh, arranged the dinner. Are you free to join us?' 'Of course I am', I replied. So it was that I met again a member of my family who will be remembered by history as a pragmatic visionary, although no one would have predicted such a success story back in 1639".

"As the dinner progressed, it became clear that Menasseh was unhappy. He felt he had not achieved everything required by destiny. I heard him say to Pinto-Lopes that Cromwell, despite being personally committed to the Jewish return, had decided that the arrangement should be informal rather than legalised, for public opinion — inflamed by certain hostile business interests — was not as favourable towards the Jews as he himself was, although other business interests thought Jewish mercantile skills would benefit the country".

"I quoted Rabbi Tarphon's famous remark from the *Ethics of the Fathers* to him: 'it is not your duty to complete the work, but neither are you free to desist from it', but he shrugged his shoulders and continued drinking the port which, as it happened, was imported from Oporto by a Marrano merchant, Aaron Rappaport (the partner of Benjamin Disraeli Pinto-Lopes), who has a warehouse at the Port of London, a short walk from the Creechurch Lane synagogue. Have you ever drunk port, by the way? Port is a new drink, created only recently by some Liverpudlians in Portugal! Those were the very first bottles of port to be exported to the land of its expatriate creators, and very good they were too. Anyway, even though the requests made in the petition were granted — for a cemetery and synagogue in the City of London — Menasseh died the following year, a disappointed man".

"My dear Racine, I was so moved by my meeting with Menasseh and the others that my commitment to the Church, never a simple matter, was weakened. You will remember that Pascal himself quotes Moses as promising in *Deuteronomy* X verse 16 and **XXX** verse 6 that God will circumcise the hearts of the Israelites. Well, I began to study the faith of my ancestors and re-circumcised (as it were) my heart in private. Thirty years later, three years ago, I began to practise my religion openly. I shall die a Jew. And now it is time for me to pray".

Malachi ben-Joseph closed his eyes and started humming. Jean Racine asked him if the tune was connected with the onset of the Sabbath. "Yes, I was humming *lecha dodi*, the hymn to the Sabbath bride. I know several tunes. This is a recent one, composed in Mantua by Salomone di Rossi in 1594, the year Ruy Lopes's great-grandfather was executed. Did you know that di Rossi became a friend of Monteverdi after he moved to Venice? Monteverdi himself is said to have been a Marrano from Ferrara, apparently changing his name from Greenberg. It is not impossible that Giorgione too was Jewish".

Trying hard to keep a straight face Racine said: "You are proving Pascal's point about the splendid brotherhood of Jews! I expect you are related to the di Rossi family too". Malachi had the grace to laugh. Resisting the temptation to mention Montaigne's mother, he embraced Racine and went upstairs to pray. He could not bring himself to admit to his friend that the di Rossis were indeed his cousins by marriage, or so it was said. Nor did he hint at a suspicion in his mind that Racine himself might have a Marrano background: it would explain some of the secrecy concerning Racine's origins, and might also have contributed to the playwright's empathy with Jewish aspirations for freedom and independence, as found in his last two plays. No, keep *shtum*, Malachi told himself, remembering a word used by Felusz Raphael, the brother-in-law of Esteban; Racine had enough potential trouble over his suspected religious beliefs without the addition of a Jewish component to the brew. In any case, he was well aware that any persecution of any group was anathema to his old student.

14.

At the opening night of *Athalie* in 1691, Malachi ben-Joseph had an honoured seat in the front row. Ten days later he was dead from a sudden heart attack at the age of seventy-two. Although Racine wrote no plays after *Athalie*, it was while walking past Malachi's house one afternoon in 1694 – perhaps three hundred yards from his own in rue Visconti — that the great writer began composing his last literary work, the four *Cantiques spirituels*. Once again, they were intended for Saint-Cyr, with music by Lully. A surviving notebook reveals that he had intended to dedicate them to "my old teacher and mentor, Malachi ben-Joseph, also known as Angelo Antoine Oltrarno. *Shalom, Abba*", but it never appeared in print, perhaps to avoid problems for the community of Port-Royal.

In 1696, Racine, himself suffering from what would later become known as the Touraine-Solent-Gole syndrome, was asked by the insomniac king (a condition the playwright had already alluded to in act two scene one of *Esther*) to calm his nerves by reading to him. Unlike previous occasions — when he read from the history of the King's reign which he had co-authored — this time Racine read to Louis from Plutarch's *Lives*, in the French translation Oltrarno had given him as a present. That night Racine thought a great deal about his late mentor. "May the memory of his name be for a blessing", he murmured to himself.

15.

"Reveal, if you can, the secrets of his soul", the dramatist wrote in *Britannicus* in 1669. Jean Racine died in 1699 and even though he was out of favour — the suspicion of Jansenism still hung over him — he wished no soul in hell.

ABOUT THE AUTHOR

Anthony Rudolf is the author of *Silent Conversations: A Reader's Life* (Seagull Books/University of Chicago Press, 2013), *European Hours: Collected Poems* (Carcanet Press, 2017) and *Journey Around My Flat* (Shearsman Books, 2021) and the translator of *Yesterday's Wilderness Kingdom* by Yves Bonnefoy (MPT Books, 2003).

Printed in Great Britain
by Amazon